My
name
is
Nathan
Lucius

My
name
is
Nathan
Lucius

—

Mark
Winkler

SOHO
CRIME

Copyright © 2015 by Mark Winkler

First published under the title *Wasted* by Kwela Books, Cape Town, 2015

First US edition published in 2018 by
Soho Press
853 Broadway
New York, NY 10003

Library of Congress Cataloging-in-Publication Data

Winkler, Mark.
My name is Nathan Lucius / Mark Winkler.
Other titles: Wasted

ISBN 978-1-61695-882-4
eISBN 978-1-61695-883-1

International paperback edition ISBN 978-1-61695-925-8
International eISBN 978-1-61695-926-5

1. Assisted suicide—Fiction. 2. Euthanasia—Fiction. I. Title
PR9369.4.W56 W37 2017 823'.92—dc23 2017011307

Interior design by Janine Agro, Soho Press, Inc.

Printed in the United States of America

10 9 8 7 6 5 4 3 2 1

For my Michelle

My
name
is
Nathan
Lucius

AFTER

MY NAME

- My name is Nathan Lucius. I sleep with the light on.
- I buy old photographs of people I don't know. I give them names and arrange them into a family tree on my wall. This means I can have a new family whenever I want.
- I'm happiest when each day is exactly like the one before.
- I like to run. I hate the beach.
- When Mrs. du Toit next door masturbates I can hear her coming behind my wall of photographs. I've never seen her husband. Maybe that's why she does it all the time. Sometimes the sound inspires me to the same. I think of her even though she is over forty.
- I work at a daily newspaper where I sell advertising space. It's a job.
- I like to drink. I like to watch TV.
- I had a girlfriend a while ago. One day I told her that I'd rather wank than have sex with her, so she left.
- My name is Nathan Lucius. I am thirty-one years old. I live in a flat in Pansyshell Park. I have no pets.

OFTEN THE NEWS IN THE MORNING

Often the news in the morning edition doesn't get much past page twelve. After that it's business and sport. Sometimes you'll find that page twelve is already in the business supplement. There are seven billion people on the planet. It worries me that the journos can only find enough stories to fill twelve pages. What a boring species we must be.

There are more ads than stories anyway. It's like the journos are there only to fill the gaps between the commercial stuff. Maybe it's enough to put them off writing past page twelve, the knowledge that you're just writing around ads for cars or margarine. It must be disheartening.

In the three years I've been here it's become harder and harder to sell ad space even though the spaces have got smaller. You measure the spaces in centimetres up and by columns across. I've always struggled to understand that. It's like measuring something in so many cubits high by so many wombats wide. My boss, Sonia, blames the bad sales on the internet. She blames most things on the internet. Child porn, global warming, the wrong election results. Sonia has been here far longer than I have. She tells me that in the old days it was piss-easy to sell a double-page spread. Those are her words. Sometimes she speaks like a sailor. Double pages used to cost as much as a small house back then. Advertisers would buy them all the time. Now we have to "add value" by "bundling" sales in the print edition with online sales. It's a carrot to get advertisers to spend money. We sell fewer double-page spreads than ever. Everyone is reading the news on their phones or their tablets or whatever. The bosses say we have to keep the print edition going. I don't know why. Me, I'd just call it a day.

In summer Sonia wears no bra and cotton tops that don't hide her long nipples. She has a great wild bush of blonde hair and little blue Renée Zellweger eyes. Before Renée got a new face, I mean.

She tells me, frequently, that her commission was so good back in the day that she didn't know what to do with her money. So she started taking drugs and ended up in rehab. The paper paid for it all. When she was straight she was very good at her job. She had to take a salary cut to pay them back. She says this was a good thing. It meant that she had less cash to blow on drugs. She tells me this mostly when we go to Eric's Bar. Clearly rehab didn't cover drinking. She tells me that the drugs are never further away than the tips of her fingers. All she has to do is reach out. Like reaching to scratch an itch that itches all the time. Counselling other people helps, she says. She sees herself in their eyes at every session. Sonia is pretty and sweet-looking. Most girls want big cow eyes. Sonia's little eyes suit her. The drug thing scares me and so do the long nipples.

When I feel like a beer and Sonia can't make it I go to Eric's Bar on my own. I've got to know Eric quite well over the years. He is an enormous mountain of a man. Sometimes when he is tired at the end of the evening he gets a waiter to reach for the drinks in the fridge under the counter. His accent is thick and German. He once wrestled for Germany in the Olympics. He was a Greco-Roman specialist and fought in the 74–84 kg category. He didn't win anything. That was a long time ago. Then life took over, he says. I suppose that life might add up by way of an extra hundred and fifty kilograms. Some people accumulate things. Even me. I accumulate photographs and money I can't spend. Eric accumulates flesh.

If it's quiet he'll draw with a pencil on a large white pad while we chat. The stuff he draws comes from his head. He'll draw kitschy Bavarian alpine scenes if he's feeling uninspired. It's actually the same scene each time. With the same mountain and the same trees and the same small-windowed house. The roof looks too big for it. Like it's trying to push the house into the ground.

Or else he'll draw wizards or witches who look like they'll hex you right off the page. Demons that threaten to drag you into the paper with them. I tell him he could be famous. He shrugs me off. He gives his witches and wizards to drinking dads to give to their kids. Long ago he pinned one of his alpine scenes to the edge of a shelf. It's gone yellow over time and the corners have curled up. I keep meaning to ask him why he doesn't replace it with a new one. He must have hundreds by now.

"Where is that?" I once asked him as he began another. As usual he'd started with an outline of the mountain. He shrugged and put his pad away.

SOMETIMES SONIA'S BOYFRIEND comes up from the newsroom to visit her. His name is Dino and he's a reporter. He has no problem with filling the spaces between ads. He is proud of the fact that he does only hard news. Crime, violence, corruption. No kittens in trees or hundredth birthdays. He is bilingual and we all know that he writes for the local Afrikaans daily on the side. It's our competition and he's not supposed to. Dino is tall and wiry. He runs marathons and climbs rocks and cycles up mountains. He doesn't drink. Sometimes he'll join us at Eric's and have an orange juice. Once some old greybeard took his face out of his whisky glass and tried to give Dino a hard time about the juice. Dino stared at him without blinking. The greybeard shut up and turned away. If I'm busy with Sonia and Dino appears I'll find a reason to go back to my desk.

He takes over the chair I've been sitting on and kind of lies on it. He splays his legs and puts his hands behind his head and generally inhabits the whole of Sonia's cubicle. I don't know how she can breathe with him in there. Even from my desk I can hear him bragging about a story he's just broken. How he's had to dodge a drug lord's bullets. How he's been getting death threats since writing about some politician or other. How he has some pet policemen in key positions who always slip him the good stories first. Today he's on about a body found in the Liesbeek River with a crossbow bolt through the chest. I suppose it's all very exciting if you're a certain kind of person. I'd like to sew his mouth shut with a curved needle and catgut.

I WAIT FOR Sonia in Eric's bar on Thursday after work. A woman comes in and sits on a stool near me. She is tall and wears a short skirt that is dark green and shiny. Her sunglasses are pushed up to keep her hair back. She orders a drink and lights a cigarette and then lights another and another and then orders a second drink and lights a ciga-rette. Three cigarettes per drink seems to be the going rate. She keeps looking at me as if she is trying to catch my eye. Something in her face tells me she has a smile waiting. I'm sure it would launch itself if I looked at her properly. I manage a glance at her crow's feet and the heavy mascara and the vertical wrinkle above her nose. I don't look her in the eye. There are a lot of people in the bar. I wish she would look at one of them instead. Her hands are older than her face. Her long legs are a bit lumpy at the thighs. I know this because she keeps crossing and uncrossing them on the bar stool. Her skirt rides up higher. I try hard not to look. The harder I try the more she does it. I haven't showered for three days.

I am talking to Eric and watching her out of the corner of my eye when she gives a little grunt and jerks up off her stool and slides to the floor. She hasn't been here long enough to be that entirely drunk. It must be something else. I go over to her and shake her around a bit. She doesn't respond. I put my ear to her mouth. It sounds like she isn't breathing. I put my forefinger to her wrist. I can't feel a pulse. I kneel and pump down with both hands on her chest. I can't remember the ratio. I pump a few more times. I put my mouth over hers and hold her nose closed and blow down her throat. I do it again and again. Then I slip my tongue into her mouth. I don't know why. She tastes of cigarettes and some sweet drink. The weirdness of pumping away at some strange woman's chest and then putting my mouth over hers makes me break a sweat. I pump. I put my mouth over hers and blow. I taste her cigarettes and her drink again. I promise myself that I will shower after my run in the morning.

Eric must have called the ambulance. Paramedics

stand over me. I'm kneeling next to the woman and gasp for breath. I can smell my sweat. I feel I deserve a break. Other people from the bar stand around. They haven't done anything. As if looking concerned will wrench her back into the land of the living. I have the woman's lipstick all over my face. I try to wipe it away with my wrist. I think she is breathing again because her eyelids flicker like she is having a bad dream. A paramedic looks at me sideways. He takes my hand off her boob. I hadn't even realised it was there. It's only then that I feel her breast in my palm. They put her on a gurney and wheel her out. I go with them to make sure they don't drop her or something on the way. After all that I feel like she's mine. Just a little bit mine. They manage to get her into the ambulance okay.

The ambulance goes screaming into the dark and I go back inside to finish my drink. Everyone starts clapping when I walk in. Next thing Eric is lining up all the drinks everyone has bought me. I look around for Sonia. She hasn't pitched. I'm happy to spend the evening with my new friends. My last memory of the evening is actually in the morning when I wake up late for work. I open my eyes and wonder if the ambulance siren has implanted itself in my brain in the form of pure agony. I put my clothes on which are mostly yesterday's. I remember that I've forgotten to shower.

SONIA CALLS ME

Sonia calls me into her office. It's not really an office at all. It's a cubicle a little bigger than mine. My coffee slops onto her desk when I put the mug down. She looks at this and scowls. She takes a breath.

"Two things," she says. Her nipples are angry. "One, we cannot be late for work. Ever. No matter what. It's a tough job, Nathan. When you're late, you make a bad impression. You hurt your sales. You piss your clients off if they're wanting a new this and an extension on that or a discount on the other and you're not here. By ten o'clock, they're frantic. They pull their bookings and also their money. We're not the only paper trying to appeal to a particular demographic. I say particular because these are the ones going digital right now. Tablets and smartphones. They read the news on the crapper without going outside to fetch the paper first. They're not renewing their subscriptions. And guess what? You don't make your targets, I get it in the neck. Worse for you, there are a million graduates working at Micky Dee's right now who would kill for your seat. Got it?"

I sip my coffee. It wants to make me vomit. Sonia's

nipples are giving me a hard-on at the same time. Hangovers always make me horny. I don't understand why. It's simply how it is. The nipples are like cocktail viennas. I wonder if they'll tear holes through Sonia's T-shirt. I want to bite them.

"And two, personal hygiene," she carries on. "Nathan, you smell. Of booze and feet and bum. Just about always. Take a fucking shower from time to time, for the love of God. There are twenty people on this floor. They have to work right next to you and you smell like a whole locker room on your own. Jesus."

I lift an arm and bury my nose in the pit. I can't help myself. I sniff. It's not pleasant. Sometimes I don't argue with Sonia. Sometimes she's right. After all these years, I've perfected my contrite face. I have a laughing face that I put on when everyone is laughing. I have a serious face for meetings and things. I have a library of other faces that I put on at appropriate moments. Or maybe it's a wardrobe. Or a closet. Whatever you call that place where you keep your faces.

"Where were you last night?" I ask. "We had an appointment." I'm going from contrite to sulky. It's not working. Sonia looks at me strangely. The viennas deflate and disappear. She sits back. Her hands move about like she's trying to draw me a picture in the air. She stops and her hands drop to her lap. "Christ, Nathan," she says.

"Thanks for coming, then," I say. "Hope you enjoyed the party."

Sonia starts waving her hands around again. "You can be such a, such a, such an absolute arsehole," she says. "Have you even checked your emails yet?"

"Sorry. I was late," I remind her.

She lifts her coffee mug. It's black with a dead smiling yellow Nirvana face on it. I once read somewhere that black ceramics are bad for you. That the glaze they use gives you cancer or something. I suppose you can get cancer from just about anything these days. Shampoo, polony, new car interiors. Sonia sips from her cancerous mug. She makes a gross face. "Three more things, Nathan. One: last night I left exactly seven seconds after you tried to stick your tongue down my throat. Two: your Sleeping Beauty is dead. Either you didn't pull off the Prince Charming thing, or she died on the way to hospital. Who cares, either way? Three: I'm trying to help you here so that I don't have to fire your arse. Get with the fucking programme. There's only so much I can do."

The news that the woman has died makes me feel weirder than I did when I was thumping on her chest. Weirder even than when I slipped my tongue in. She died and then I thought I'd made her alive with my Boy Scout first-aid. With all the technology of the twenty-first cen- tury plugged into her she died again. For good. Or maybe she'd just stayed as dead as she was in the first place. The twitching eyelids a last bit of electricity. Like a chicken with its head cut off. She was probably dead when I stuck my tongue in her mouth.

I DON'T DISLIKE women. I just don't like what they can do to me. What they *could* do to me. Even when what they're doing is precisely nothing. So I like them, mostly. I like that my boss is a woman. I like that we're friends. I don't like that she could fire me. I like that Mrs. du Toit from next door is a woman. I like that she sounds like one.

I liked the taste of the dead lady who may or may not have been properly dead.

Still, women are different to men. They expect things. Like how was I supposed to remember after forty-eight free drinks that Sonia had been at Eric's. That I'd tried to get off with her.

So anyway. Friday creeps to a close. My hangover is just about gone. I know how to make what's left of it disappear. I go to Sonia's cubicle to see if she wants a drink at Eric's. Her laptop is missing from its plastic stand and her desk is all squared up. The space between the three-and-a-half walls of grey fabric smells like her. Like stationery and old lunch and new perfume. Something makes me want to sniff the seat of her chair. I don't.

I go to Eric's anyway. When I get there I don't want to

go in. It's too full of hairy men and overweight women. Through the window I can see that the men are talking too much and saying too little. The women show too much and talk even more. I can see that Eric is too busy to chat. He is sweating. I hope he never has a heart attack while I'm visiting. I don't feel like fighting my way to the bar for a chance not to chat to Eric. The thought of Eric having a heart attack makes up my mind. My mouth over his and the thumping on the blubber. The sweat on his top lip. I might just make Madge's before she closes, so I start jogging. My head starts to pound again, in time with my footfalls now. I turn around and walk back up St. George's Mall.

Madge is at her shop, about to lock up for the night.

"Hi Madge," I say. She looks at me and shoots the bolt on the security gate. She threads the shackle of an enormous lock through the loop and snaps it shut.

"Na-than!" she sings and flings her arms open. The sleeves of her hippie Indian dress flap like thin wings. She wears her usual headband. It ties up a bundle of fake hair. I know it's fake because sometimes when I visit her she closes the shop and removes it so that she can scratch at the few wisps left on her scalp. Madge has cancer and will be dead soon. She plans to be Madge until the last, she's told me. If that takes wigs and lipstick then there it is. She puckers her bright red lips as I come closer. The wrinkles draw the eye to the brilliant cloaca of her mouth. I dodge it at the last moment and kiss her on the cheek. She has a big silver bauble on a chain around her neck. It presses into my sternum as she hugs. She is stronger than she looks.

She steps back and keeps her bony hands on my shoulders. Through the scrawniness and the sunken skin I can see the beauty she once was. "You may walk with me as long as you don't ask how I am," she says. She loops her arm into mine.

"How are you, Madge?" I ask.

She lifts a shoulder. Lets it drop. "Shit," she says. "Truly, truly shit." Then she brightens. "I got some new photographs in today. You should come around and see them."

It's hard not to like Madge.

I WAKE UP BEFORE

I wake up before the alarm goes off. My head is clear. My brain is as sharp as the sun coming through the window. I don't do curtains. I pull on my running gear. It's manky enough. I take the stairs in case I meet another early riser in the lift. I stretch. I'm dying to get on the road. It's worth stretching properly before a run. The first four Ks are always the hardest. They're even harder if you haven't loosened up.

I run up the short street behind my block and join Kloof Nek Road. I turn left up the steepness. Once I'm done with its zigging ascent I head left at the circle at the summit and run up past the cable station. Tafelberg Road takes me along the face of Table Mountain. I turn around at the ravine that divides the monolith of the mountain from Devil's Peak. It's already a February scorcher. The morning has the potential of an oven just turned on. In an hour or so it will be too hot to run.

When I get home I take the stairs again. I smell worse than before. I don't want to stink up the lift. On the fourth-floor landing I promise promise promise myself a shower. The tiles are covered with crusty grey swirls. It's revolting.

I throw dishwashing liquid on it and scrub with the toilet brush. I let the scum rinse away while the water warms up. The tiles look better. The grouting remains black.

By the time I am out of the shower my fingers have wrinkled. I scrub at my hair with the towel. I should cut it some time. I pull on a T-shirt. My hair soaks the back of it down to my shoulder blades. The shower has made me feel lighter somehow. I take my running gear and two weeks' worth of dirty laundry and stuff it into a duffel bag. I take the lift and walk down the hill. I drop the bag at the laundrette on Kloof Street. You can self-service if you want, or you can leave it with the attendant. She knows me. I dump my bag on the counter. Her shoulders slump. I wonder if her life is more or less interesting than mine. Across the road is one of those old cafés that sells everything from soft drinks and newspapers to spices and second-hand novels. Salie's is one of the few shops to have survived petrol-station convenience stores and late-night 7-Elevens. I wait for Salie to warm my sausage roll in his microwave. There's a smell of dust and curry and old fruit and paper. I breathe it in. It's homely and familiar and almost edible. I pay for the sausage roll and the Sparberry that will help wash it down.

It's past opening time when I get to Madge's. The door to her shop is locked. Sometimes she'll close it when she feels like a cup of tea. It's time to bugger the customers, she says every time. It's not even nine-thirty. It's too early for her to have tea. I peer through the security bars. I try to make her out beyond the second-hand furniture that clutters the place. Antique, Madge calls her wares. By her own admission she wouldn't know Regency from Bauhaus. I can't see her through the security bars or beyond the shapes inside. I remember that she wasn't well last evening. I remember that I'd walked with her a while. The memory tries to lead on to the next one. There's nothing there. I'm certain I went home. The hangover I didn't have this morning tells me I didn't go back to Eric's. I try to picture myself approaching Pansyshell Park in the gathering dark. I try to remember opening my door and putting on the TV. I suppose there's nothing much worth remembering about my evening.

I can't see Madge. Then I hear her. "Darling!" she sings. She is crossing St. George's Mall. The Somalis and Nigerians are already at their stalls under the plane trees. She's late. I wonder if she's had a bad night. She has a bunch of keys in her hand and a fantastic pink hat on her head. A dress of bright florals swirls around her bones. She kisses the air with her red lips. She takes a tress of my hair in her hand and holds it to her nose. "So clean!" she says. "If I were still a lass, then who knows?" She fiddles with her keys. There are two locks to be undone. One on the shackle of the security gate and the other on the door of the shop. Why she has a bunch of twenty or so keys I wouldn't know.

I make tea in the alcove behind the veneered book-shelves. At the end of the alcove is a door. I open it to allow some of the mustiness and mildew to escape. Madge keeps it closed for security reasons. It opens onto a gated alley. I've told her often enough that it's safe to have it open.

Madge puts out two bone china cups. They are mis-matched and chipped and so are the saucers. She bends slowly to scrabble in a cupboard. "Ooh, cookies," she says and takes out a box of Romany Creams. I wonder how long they've been in there. Antiques themselves. She goes into the shop ahead of me. Her neck is craned forward. At the top of her spine, the beginnings of a hump. I can see her vertebrae lined up like knuckles in her neck.

We sit. She's in a Quaker-style rocking chair. I'm on a tall bar stool with a leatherette seat and tarnished chrome legs. One of the little rubber feet is missing. She raises her cup towards the stool. "Twenties," she says, "Art Deco. Very rare."

We drink our tea. I take a biscuit to be polite. It is soft and gently rancid. She bitches about her nephew who has just lost his business. Again. She tells me she is feeling a little better this morning. After a long day, who knows how she'll be feeling? She can't tell whether it's the cancer or the drugs that make her feel so ill. Then she switches to drama mode.

"Goodness!" she shrieks. "I nearly forgot why you're here." She struggles from her chair and tries to pick up an old photo album from the counter.

"Here, let me."

I put it on my lap and turn its stiff leaves. Either the weight on my groin or the contents give me the beginnings of a hard-on. I don't know. I buy all my photographs from Madge. Long ago I tried to buy the framed image of a young man on her desk. His weasely look made him interesting. The perfect black sheep for my family. The picture was of her nephew. NFS. Not For Sale. The frame didn't have a stand and leant against an old clothing iron. It's called an "iron" because originally they were made of iron. You had to put live embers into it to heat it up. The nephew is still there, leering out of the frame like a pimp or a car salesman.

Looking through the album is not like flicking through a magazine at the dentist's. Every image on every page carries its own fraction of the weight of the world. The weight of births and unions and deaths. Pain and love and hope and failure. Each portrait gives the subject a sense of purpose. Proclaiming that they're here because they're meant to be. That their drawing of breath and their dropping of faeces and their opinions and ideas and prejudices were preordained. Important. That their footfalls and elbow-nudges as they made their way across the great spinning earth would make a difference. That thing we all think, that we're significant, that we matter. When in reality we're forgotten before we're born. When our footprints are so shallow they disappear long before we die. Still we believe we mean something. Madge's album is the album of every person who ever lived. Even though it barely covers half a century. Each face, each pose tells a wordless story. The sum of untold details. What's really important is the end result. There are many ways to lose a leg. Hundreds of reasons to wear a frown. A thousand ways to win a medal. Even more to get married. What's important is where we end up. *Who* we end up.

That's what we think. It's not, really.

I never buy photos that are annotated. The comments ruin the story. They mean it's already half-told. I need to start my stories from scratch. Tabula rasa. I can smell shampoo in my hair. I comb it behind my ears with my fingers. The album starts off Edwardian, stretches into the twenties, the thirties. It begins to thin out in the forties. Only a few of the pictures were taken in the fifties. As if libidos had waned. Or a slow plague had taken hold. The photos are sepia, black and white, scalloped at the edges, some of them. Small white triangles at the corners fix the photos to the black pages. There are couples and singles and families and priests and soldiers and dowagers and patriarchs. Hardly anyone smiles. The women are sexless.

The men have laughable moustaches. Unhygienic, probably. Soaked with soup and hung with bits of lunch. The album has not a word written in it, not a single date.

It's perfect.

I close it and a photograph falls to the floor. A young woman. In colour. She's wearing sunglasses and a sleeveless dress and is leaning against the fender of a car. The hair says sixties, early seventies perhaps. Some colour has leached from the print and the red of her dress has a blue tinge as does the green of the car. The sky is flat and thin. Jutting into the image is the tail of a light aircraft. A Cessna or a Piper or something. Only half of the registration code is visible. The woman is looking slightly to the left. In spite of the big sunglasses, I know there's sadness in her eyes. She is posing and the pose is tense. She doesn't want to be photographed. She looks out at something that's not really there. She could be looking into a past of indecision. Into a future that's the consequence. The wind is blowing her hair back. I think she should be wearing a Princess Grace scarf. She isn't. Beyond the aeroplane tail, there's the blur of a windsock. I'm looking at her from the precise perspective of a handsome young man holding his new Leica. Pilots, both. Flying was the sport of the young and rich back then.

She is beautiful.

"I'll buy her," I tell Madge.

Madge takes a slightly used tissue from under her watch strap and hands it to me. I dab at my eyes.

"You know the deal," Madge says. "All for one, one for all." We agreed long ago never to split families of photographs. We agreed that nothing would be sadder. There's no guarantee that the woman at the airfield belongs to the album at all. I know that at some time there will be space for the rest of them among the family on my wall. Man with Beard and Sour Woman, who begat Son in Uniform, who begat Swaddled Babe with Young Nurse the day before he left for Tripoli. Pouch-eyed Priest and Plump Marm, Playboy with Racehorse, the Bastard Triplets in their crib, crying as Mannequin in Polka Dot Blouse smiles over them. At the end of them, Woman in the Red Dress. And then me, starting all over again.

I GET INTO THE LIFT AND IT FILLS UP

I get into the lift and it fills up with the smell of shampoo and deodorant and soap. It's me. I'm not used to it. The album is under my arm. The woman in the red dress is in my top pocket. I don't want her to fall out and blow away. I step out of the lift. Mrs. du Toit's butt is pointed at me. She's only just moved in. Her name must be Mrs. du Toit. It's what it says on her postbox.

Her butt is a good size and a good shape. She is bent over and trying to push something big and white towards her flat. It looks like a washing machine. The bubble wrap makes it hard to tell. Mrs. du Toit is wearing tight white leggings that end halfway down her calves. Her calves are pale and strong. Her white top has a streak of sweat down the spine. Her pushing hardly moves the thing. The white high heels aren't helping. She stands up and takes a big breath. Her shoulders droop. For a moment her hands are on her hips. She puts them on the white thing. Her head droops too. It's not hard to see she has no idea of how to get the thing into her flat.

"Let me help you with that," I say. She hasn't heard me approach and jerks around. Her eyes are wet with frustration. I don't really want to help her. I want to get inside and explore my new photographs. I can hardly step around her without offering.

"Thank you," she says. "They just left it here and disappeared." She sniffs damply. She turns away and wipes her eyes with the heel of a hand. Leaves a smear of mascara at the corners, Cleopatra style.

"I'll just put this down," I say. I open the door of my flat a crack and slip in sideways. I close it behind me. I don't want Mrs. du Toit to see inside. Nobody has ever been in here. Other than me, of course. There's no reason to change that now. I put the album on my couch. I take the woman in the red dress from my pocket and slip her under the front cover. It's all I can do not to close the door on Mrs. Du Toit and her white machine. There is far more important stuff to do.

WE WRESTLE THE thing into her flat. I still don't know if it's a washing machine or a tumble dryer or a dishwasher or whatever. I'm sweating. So is Mrs. du Toit. I'm going to have to have another shower soon. Droplets are clinging to the hairs on Mrs. du Toit's top lip. She wipes them away, with the back of her wrist this time. The white thing is standing in the middle of her flat. It's a bigger flat than mine. There's a doorway I don't have, and no bed in the middle of the space.

"Shoo," she says. She would probably have spelt it sjoe. "Can I get you something to drink?"

I'm in a quandary. Mrs. Du Toit wants to reward me for my help. My best reward would be to be released to my flat.

I'm parched.

"I'm good, thanks," I say.

Mrs. Du Toit goes to her fridge and takes a plastic water bottle from a shelf. She unscrews it and drinks from it. The mouth of the bottle is wide. Water runs down her chin. It streaks her neck and wets her top at the collarbones. It's like the start of a porn movie. The housewife and the plumber.

"Actually, some of that water would be great."

You never know.

She reaches for a glass in a cupboard. Her top is sleeveless. I can see that it's been a while since she's shaved. She fills the glass from the bottle.

"Adele," she says as she hands me the glass. For a moment I think it's some kind of toast.

"Nathan," I say.

"Next-door Nathan," she says. I feel the blood draining from my face. She knows I listen to her. She tosses her head back and laughs. I can see the silver of fillings. Mercury makes you mad. Ask any hatter. Her black hair is heavy with sweat. It's dyed, I'm sure. Up close she looks like there should be streaks of grey in it. With the makeup gone cats-eye she looks a tiny bit deranged. I don't understand why she's laughing. I put on my smiling face. "Let's get this baby going," she says and gives the white thing an affectionate kick. As if it were an old family dog.

IT'S A TUMBLE dryer and Adele du Toit wants it in the bathroom. We have to walk the machine through the doorway into her bedroom before we get to the bathroom. She hasn't made the bed. The duvet is piled on one side. I can see the shape of her on the sheet. There's no husband shape next to it. There's a smell of a living thing in the room. The living thing is her. I suppose my bedroom has its own smell too. In fact I'm certain it has. A canine smell. Or worse, lupine. Hyena-ish. On the other side of the wall is my flat. The bedroom isn't very big. First we have to push her bed against the window. Then we walk the dryer into the bathroom past the bed. The bathroom is ridiculously small. It's ridiculously hot. We tear bubble wrap from the dryer. Then we have to wedge the dryer into a gap between the washing machine and the vanity stand. The gap looks too tight. It almost is. I have no idea of how to make the thing work. She finds the manual. It reads like it's been translated from Korean to French to Swedish to English. From the diagrams it looks like I simply have to plug it in. I see straight off that we have to pull the dryer out again so that I can fiddle with the cord and the plug behind it. She laughs again, throws her head back. Sweaty drops fall from her onto my forearms, my legs. My face. I wonder if she does herself here or in the bedroom. Maybe both. The holes of the wall socket have rust in them. It's not easy to force the plug in. She stops me when I want to turn the machine on to see if it works. She squats down to transfer wet items from the washing machine to the mouth of the dryer. I see clothes, towels, underwear. I can see down her crack as she squats. There's pale hair at the base of her spine. She closes the dryer. With a flourish, she invites me to switch it on. It works. It sounds like a jet as it churns her laundry into a slow kaleidoscope of colour.

"Celebration!" she bellows. She takes me by the arm and hurries me out of the bathroom. Through the bedroom. She opens the fridge and takes out a bottle of champagne. It's not actually champagne. Real champagne comes from France. This is from Franschhoek. We drink it. The whole bottle in like twenty minutes. I could drink a lot more. Mrs. du Toit sits on the couch opposite me. Her shoes are on the floor. She's swinging her glass from her fingers and looking at me. Swing, swing, look, look. I can't make out what her face means. All I know is it's making me horny. Then she rolls her eyes and her face goes back to normal. She gets up and puts her glass in the sink. She kind of just stands there. She crosses her arms and looks at her toes.

They flex up and down. I realise what her face meant. By now it means something else.

I go to my flat. It's really just a room with a bed, couch and kitchen all in one. I sniff the air and try to smell me in the air. I can't. I open the album. The urgency has gone. And anyway I'm pretty fucking pissed off with myself. I close it again. Lie on the bed. Wrap myself in the doggy fug of the sheets. It's time they were changed. Through the wall I hear Adel Du Toit's tumble-dryer rumble like an oncoming train. I strain to hear something else from next door. There's nothing.

I SPEND MOST OF SUNDAY WAITING

I spend most of Sunday waiting for Monday. Sometimes that's all Sundays are good for.

On Monday I hear from Madge. She's left a message on my phone. She wants me to drop in after work, her voice says. She wants to tell me something. The message came in at around two in the morning. Sonia is still sulking. It's thirty degrees Celsius outside and she's wearing some kind of military jacket. The jacket says that she means business. We have a standing meeting on Mondays. A review of who's been selling what. It's not looking good. Sonia glares at her sales team, me included. Hers is a classical passive-aggressive management style. I know she'll smile sweetly before she berates us about our sales. Yumna enters the boardroom last. She's late. She has a Vida coffee and a giant muffin in her hands.

Here comes the smile.

"Hungry, sweetheart?" Sonia says to her. The smile spreads. Yumna smiles back and widens her eyes and nods. So innocent. You'd think she'd have learnt by now. "Don't you think it would benefit all of us if you were hungry on your own time? Instead of expecting everyone to wait for you?"

Yumna's smile dissolves. She sits and looks down at the desk and mumbles something.

I don't have to listen to Sonia. Two things, three things, five things. We're short of our targets, the paper is under increasing pressure, our web offering isn't yet strong enough to compensate. Generally we're all a bunch of lazy arseholes who are completely out of touch with the real world. Three more things. And so on. Yumna stares at the muffin on the table. I replay Madge's message in my head. She's left me messages at odd hours before. Perhaps I'm imagining a difference in her voice this time. Some tonal shift. Or a slurring as if she was drunk. I hold my phone under the table and text her to see if she's okay. I don't expect a reply. I know she only ever turns her cellphone on when she needs to make a call.

Sonia breaks off the bollocking of her crew. The smile returns. "Nathan? Something more important on the go?"

"Sorry, family issues." I hit send and put the phone on the table. Sonia glares at me. She knows that I have as much to do with family as penguins do with polar bears. At least she has the grace not to raise this. Many people don't know that penguins and polar bears live at opposite ends of the world. That they have about as much in common as macaques and English sheepdogs. Sonia finishes the meeting by congratulating Sarel on securing a big place-ment. It's her idea of motivation. To end on a thirty-second positive after a half-hour's bollocking. All it does is piss everyone else off. Sarel is younger than me. He's spends a lot of time at the gym. He's partial to the kind of blond highlights beloved of twink gays and Afrikaans rugby players. How he's convinced anyone to place even a classified ad in that accent of his is beyond me.

Sonia lets us go. I'm behind her as we walk to our cubicles. I put on my silly-cheerful face. "Morning, boss," I say. She doesn't turn around. She'll get over it. Just not right now, I guess.

I have an email message from Ally. Almost sixty and still heads up media at a big ad agency. Most are finished by then. Fried, broken. Looking far older than they actually are. Opening coffee shops or living in Kalk Bay with their cats. For some reason Ally always gets hold of me personally when she has something big on the way. I call her. There's an English bank that's bought big chunks of a South African one, she tells me. More than that she's not allowed to say. I don't care who's bought whom. She tells me that their ad agency has commissioned a six-week launch campaign for the rebranding. Cover wraps and double-page spreads for starters, full pages to follow. Page takeovers and rich media to dominate the financial section of our website. She starts talking media-strategist stuff like ARs and ROI and reach and frequency. All I want from her is a budget and a brief. I let her talk. It's important to make her feel important. A shadow passes over my desk. Dino's on his way to visit Sonia. Even though it's Monday and Mondays are always frantic, I know she'll let him lie in her chair. He'll fill her cubicle with armpits and noise for half an hour or so. The crossbow death was a Chinese mafia hit, Dino starts saying. The cops have confirmed it. He can't quote them just yet. He's hardly greeted her. Blah blah blah he goes. Yak yak yak. If he doesn't shut up I'm going to miss the point where I have to respond to Ally. I stand up with the phone wedged between my ear and my shoulder. Dino's natter skips a syllable as I poke my head over the cubicle divider. Then he starts yapping again. I raise a hand, point to the phone on my shoulder, put a finger to my lips. Sonia looks around to see what's going on. I stick my tongue out at her. Dino shuts up and I sit down.

Ally gives me the budget. It's probably good that I'm sitting again. Sonia may remember campaigns with budgets that size. I don't. Ally mails her brief to me while she's talking. Says she knows it's crazy timing. Says she really needs a preliminary proposal first thing in the morning to present to the client and the agency.

It's not crazy. It's impossible.

No problem, I say.

What's with ad agencies, I wonder. Everything is always a last-minute panic. As though every job is a total surprise to them. As though the people who populate the agencies were born at exactly five that morning. Every morning. Or as if years of experience were erased by a simple night's sleep and they had to start each day from scratch. Dino's shadow goes the other way as Ally says goodbye. He must be bored with not talking. Sonia comes to stand at the entrance to my cubicle. She has taken off her jacket and stands with her arms crossed under her boobs. They're not very big. I can see she's impatient. I prolong the goodbyes. Then I end the call and dial Tammy at reception.

"What was that all about?" Sonia asks.

I hold my hand up. I wait for Tammy to answer. I tell her to put my calls through to Yumna. I know that will make Sonia bristle. I put the phone down and lean back in my chair and put my hands behind my head, Dino style. I swivel to face Sonia. Splay my legs.

"Wow," I say.

"Wow what?" she says. She's starting to look like she needs to pee.

I purse my lips. Let out a long slow puff. "I'm going to need your help with this," I tell her.

"With fucking *what*?" she says. I smile and turn back to my computer and open the Excel document that Ally has sent me. I hit the print button. Close the document. Stand and squeeze myself past Sonia. Go and wait at the printer. Sonia follows me. Her arms are still crossed. I whistle softly as I wait. Drum on the beige plastic of the printer with my fingernails. They're not as clean as they might be. I make a fuss of gathering the pages together. I staple them at a corner. For once the stapler actually has staples in it. Sonia seems about to burst.

"Come," I say. She follows me to the boardroom. I close the door.

"Christ on a crutch, Nathan."

I point to a chair. She sits down. I flick through the printout as I walk round the table. Raise my eyebrows and shake my head. I sit opposite her and toss the papers across the table. She doesn't go through them. Just stares at the summary on the cover page. There come the nipples.

"Wow," she says.

IT'S JUST GONE nine-thirty. The only way to finish the proposal is to work through the night. I call Madge. For a long time there's no answer. The phone cuts off. My scrotum shrivels. I dial again.

"Hello?" she says. Her voice catches on the o. She clears her throat. I tell her that I won't be able to visit her today. "Oh, that's fine," she says. "It's not a big deal." I can hear that it is, though. On any other Monday I would have snuck out to see her. The shop is just down the way, two minutes' walk if you're dawdling. I hardly ever have the urge to prove myself to my employers. I know that when I do I'd better make the most of it.

Sonia ropes in Sarel. I'm happy for him to be working on my commission. I give him the digital stuff to do. It's complicated and boring. Mostly I don't get it. As soon as I think I've got it, everything changes again.

At seven Dino comes down. Finds the three of us in the boardroom. We're hunched over laptops. There are papers all over the table. We've got a long way to go. Already we're taking turns at making coffee. We use clean mugs each time. There's a small army of dirty ones at the end of the table. Soon there'll be a standoff. Once there are no more clean mugs, the next coffee-maker is going to have to wash some old ones.

Dino surveys the chaos. "What are you kids up to?"

Sarel's eyes are fixed on his laptop. Sonia looks up blankly. She does that when she's concentrating on something.

"Paying your salary," I say.

Sonia flicks a look at me.

"Good," Dino says. I'm impressed that he doesn't get all defensive. "Have fun," he says.

I look at Sonia. She's staring at her laptop. I know she can feel me looking at her.

At eleven Sonia orders pizza. I suggest a six-pack or two as a side order. Sonia snorts and orders a two-litre Coke.

Just after two Sarel asks a question about audience

ratings. He says "arse" instead of ARs. Not even the most junior person would make a mistake like that. Sonia and I know it's just the exhaustion. We all start giggling like kids. Not because arse is a rude word. It's even funnier because he said, "What are the arse?" English verbs and subjects not agreeing is a very Afrikaans thing. It takes a while before we stop laughing. We have tears running down our faces. When we stop we're all a little embarrassed. Our defences have dropped far lower than we'd have liked. Sarel's mistake wasn't that funny.

Just before four Sonia loses the standoff and goes to wash mugs.

By seven-thirty nothing is funny any more. Sarel nods off as we're reviewing the proposal. Sonia snaps at him to grow up. We struggle to tell if the proposal is good or bad or ugly. I call Ally and she answers the phone half-asleep. I tell her we're about to send the proposal and that she needs to go over it right away and get back to us if she wants anything changed before her meeting. I email her the document. We wait. If I have another cup of coffee I'm going to throw up. By nine we've heard nothing from her. I call her cellphone. It's off. I call the office number. The receptionist sounds like she had a good night's sleep. All perky and friendly. She says that Ally is in a meeting. I leave a message for her. Ally phones at ten. Says that she's received the proposal. Says she hasn't had time to go over it. It's not a problem, she says. The client presentation has been postponed to Wednesday. The breeziness in her voice makes me want to reach through the phone and do terrible things to her. I'm thinking Freddy Krueger. My job is something I deal with. It's like eating or shitting. You do it because you do it. Sometimes you get caught short. Sometimes I thoroughly hate it. I put my phone down. "It's a pleasure," I say to it.

I'm sure Sonia's going to make it all my fault. She doesn't. She's bigger than that. She's been through this before.

"Fucking bitch," Sonia says. "Let's go home." Sarel has fallen asleep in Dino's chair. He isn't a snorer. Sonia kicks him on the ankle. He jerks as he wakes up.

As I leave the building I realise that something has happened to me. The world is sharp and bright. The leaves of the trees in the mall are green crystals in some kind of luminous fluid. The fluid makes every colour brighter. Every shape clearer. The nausea of a sleepless night slides away from me. I could prove a theorem right now. Win a court case. Understand wormholes. It's not the first time I've stayed up all night. I know the lucidity will pass soon enough.

I visit Madge before it does. I need to make amends for standing her up. Her security gate is open. The door behind it is locked. I press the bell. Hear a chime. I wait. If she'd gone out she would have locked the gate. I ring again. Nothing. I go down St. George's, turn left into Church Street. Halfway between Church and Burg is the gate to the back alley. Madge gave me two keys after she learnt that the cancer wouldn't go away. "I don't want to be found three-quarters rotten after three days," she'd said. One key opens the lock on the alleyway gate. The alley is only slightly wider than my shoulders. The other key opens the back door to her shop. It's darker in the shop than in the alley. I can hear Satie's weird piano from inside. The piece ends and starts again. For a few moments I can see nothing.

Then I see Madge sitting in her rocking chair. She has a hand in her lap. The other hangs over the armrest and points to the floor. Her head lolls on a shoulder. Fuck no, I think. What are you supposed to do? Run out waving your arms and calling people. Like Tintin, Help, help! Au secours, au secours! I go up to her. I put my ear close to her face. I hear her breathe. Soft and regular and smelling of medicine and sleep and sour stuff. All the tiredness of the night floods back into me. I take her shoulder. It's made of little panels and plates of bone.

"Madge," I say.

She looks around as if she has woken up on the ocean floor. Her eyes find me and try to focus. She has been drooling in her sleep. It's left dark patches on the orange scarf around her neck. She reaches out a hand. She takes my arm. Her hand is dry and cold.

"Nate," she whispers. "I was dreaming."

"What were you dreaming of?"

She blinks. "I don't know," she says. "Goodness." I stand gaping. She slides the tissue from under her watch strap and dabs at the side of her face. "Dribbling like an imbecile," she says.

"Happens to the best of us," I say. The words are empty. They don't help her embarrassment. I offer to make tea. She accepts, probably to give herself time to compose herself. I go to the kitchen and put on the kettle. I bring out the cracked cups and a little jug of milk. She's standing beside her chair with her hands clutching her sides. As if she's trying to hold in the pain. She looks towards the door. Shakes her head.

"Bugger the customers," she says and sits down.

I pour the tea, babble about the night's work. Moan about the irritation of the postponement after all the effort we'd put in.

Then I remember that she wanted to tell me something. I ask her what it was. She picks up her cup. She tells me.

I'VE HAD A LIFE THAT'S BEEN AMAZING

"I've had a life that's been amazing, both for the experiences I've had and because of its ordinariness," Madge says. I'm not liking the past tense. My cup has a network of fine cracks on it. I wonder why the tea doesn't leak through them. "And now I've had enough."

I look up at her and she's smiling. It's the kind of smile you have when you've achieved an almightily brilliant solution to a problem. Like deciding to consolidate your debt. Or to buy a house. Or to get married. I've never had to do any of those things. I'm just saying.

"The trouble is, I can't," she says.

I blink. The all-nighter is getting to me. I'm not following.

"I can't die, Nathan." She sips her tea and smiles. "I'm sicker than Jesus on the cross and every day I get sicker." There's no self-pity, just fact. "I've stopped taking the drugs and seeing the doctor. Every day the pain is worse. I understand why cancer is a crab. It's got claws, and every day it tears more pieces out of me. Just little bits. Just enough to increase the pain and the humiliation. Not quite enough to finish me off."

She puts her tea down. She stands up and presents her

profile to me. She smacks the top of her butt with a hand. "Do you think my bum looks big in this?" she says. Again I am lost. Madge has never had a big bum. She laughs. She pats herself again. "Incontinence knickers, Nate. There's nothing about my body I can trust any more. Look." She points to an antique chamber pot under her rocking chair. I'd never noticed it. There are a lot of things in her shop I've never seen before. "NFS," she says. "Not For Sale. Strictly FMP. For My Puke. Because when I need to, there's no time to run for the john. Not fun when you're in the salad aisle at Woolworths." She sits down. "And when I get home and take off my happy clothes"—she picks at her cerise sleeves and the puckered cloth flowers on the bodice—"I peel off my giant adult nappy, not sure what I'll find in there."

She lifts her cup and puts it down again. She looks hard at me.

"If it's full, I lie on my back on the floor with a big plastic bowl of soapy water next to me. Then I raise my legs like a baby and wash myself. Sometimes I miss a few spots." She takes her tissue from her watchstrap. She hands it to me. It's still wet with her drool. I don't care. "The crab is here," she says and puts a hand on her abdomen. "And here." She moves her hand to cover her liver. She moves it to the left. "Here." She places her hand on one breast and then the other. "Here and here." She puts two fingers on her temple. "Soon it will be here. And still I can't die. I very much want to die before it gets here." She taps the fingers against her skull. Hard. She drops her hand to her lap. I look at her. She's never spoken of her cancer like this. I haven't slept for almost thirty hours. It's not helping me in any way at all. My bitching about working through the night comes back. There's nothing like a bit of perspective to make you blush. Madge doesn't notice.

"So," she says, "I'd like you to help me." She drains her teacup.

"What do you want me to do?" I ask.

"Kill me, Nate," she says. "Kill me." She puts down her cup. Looks at me. Her eyes are flat and cold as a seagull's. "You love me, don't you?"

SO I WAS LOOKING FOR A SANDWICH

So I was looking for a sandwich at lunchtime when I first met Madge. There was a recliner outside her shop. She was lying in it. The recliner had simple chrome lines and black leather upholstery. It had a sign saying "Special, Biedermeier, R5000." The sign was written in black marker on exam-pad paper with punched holes along one side. It was stuck to the armrest with the kind of tape that is yellowish and shiny. Madge was smoking a long thin cigarette. The cigarette was in a long thin holder. Her eyes were closed. As if that cigarette was the best thing she'd ever experienced. She was dressed almost like a twenties flapper. The North Star high-tops spoiled the effect. I couldn't help myself. I stopped.

"You're a hundred years out," I said.

"I beg your pardon?"

"I said, you're a hundred years out."

She blew out a thin stream of smoke that feathered into the air. Then she laughed. "I thought you said I'm a hundred years *old*," she said. "I was about to beat you up."

I laughed because she did. She *was* old. Not that old. "That chair," I said. "It's early twentieth century. Biedermeier was early nineteenth."

She looked down at the chair, left and right. As though the new information might make it suddenly collapse. "Who would have thought," she said. "I suppose I like the word. Biedermeier. Germanic. Clean, cold lines. Expensive. And fucking uncomfortable, actually."

"It's a Le Corbusier," I said. "Or close. If it was real, it would be worth a lot more than five grand. It's shiny and the leather looks good, so it's probably a reproduction. Five grand should be fair."

"Do you like tea?" Madge asked.

I LIKED MADGE. She always gave me the time of day. She fed me tea and biscuits. I'd have preferred coffee. I didn't say so. I liked that she didn't expect an autobiography out of me. I liked that she didn't seem to care where I came from or where I didn't. Or where I was going. She asked about the things in her shop. I could place some of them. Others I couldn't. Like the pointy-tit African thing that was attached to some kind of lyre or violin. And the dragon-leg Chinese table. Maybe they were dogs and not dragons. Who knows? Madge wrote notes in a diary that was four years out of date. The diary was tiny and had a blue plastic cover with a white bank logo on it. The bank wasn't even around any more. Sometimes she would point out something herself and get it dead right. She was much more interesting than media sales. Selling ad space is always the same. Madge was always a surprise.

"How come you know so much about antiques?" she asked.

"I don't know," I said. "How come you know so little?"

BEFORE MADGE GOT sick, I'd visit her two or three times a week. We started going on buying trips together. We'd go to Swellendam and Tulbagh and Stanford. We'd try to convince farmers and shop owners to relinquish their treasures more cheaply than they wanted to. We'd pile our pickings in the back of her old Variant. Madge paid with cheques that would bounce a week later. She was younger then. Sellers often had to jumpstart her car. Just to make us go away.

Sometimes we'd have to share rooms. I'd spy on her from under the sheets. I'd sort myself out after she'd fallen asleep. Mostly people thought I was her son. In the middle of a negotiation she'd play it up and put an arm around me and make a comment about varsity fees. How outrageous they were. She would sometimes carry on even after a discount had been agreed. The enamelled signs and the oil canisters. The drop-side tables and padlocked bibles. The ship's lanterns, jonkmanskaste, hat stands, Welsh dressers, rocking chairs.

And then the cancer came. Our buying trips stopped.

She had a shop full of shit anyway. There was more stuff in storage units in Woodstock. Her hair fell out. She lost twenty kilograms and put on twenty years. I suppose she thought that the shop's contents and the stuff in storage would last until she died. I began to visit her more often. Lunchtimes. After work. Saturday mornings, sometimes.

One night I couldn't sleep because I was trying to work out how I could make myself not like her any more. She was going to die sooner or later. I didn't want it to hurt. Me, I mean. It's easier when the person who goes away is someone you don't like. Because you just don't like them. Not because you don't *want* to like them. I began to plot a way to make Madge hate me. I gave up. It was much harder than trying to make Eric hate me. Or Sonia, which would have been easy enough. I seemed to be succeeding with Sonia anyway. Madge and I talked about chemotherapy. We talked about antiques that weren't, and obscure books and strange movies. It was nice to be an undergrad again. We talked about wigs and scarves. This naturally led to conversations about transvestites and ladymen. I laughed when Madge did. We talked about today. What was missing was any demands on me. I liked that especially.

I DECIDE TO WALK HOME

I decide to walk home after I leave Madge and her theories of love and killing. Usually I take a taxi. A tuk-tuk, actually. They're stinky little three-wheeled things. The hill up to Pansyshell Park tests the limits of their ability. There's always a great buzzing. You could probably walk faster. The blue smoke sucks back into the cabin where the passengers sit. The greasiness of the tuk-tuk's two-stroke. There are no-smoking stickers in the little cabin. I can't be the only one who sees the irony in this.

The brightness returns as I walk. It's a photoshopped world. Everything is HD. The cars. The shop signs. At Café Paradiso there are the kind of people I'm not. Enjoying hard-to-pronounce lunches in neon clothing on a Tuesday. Glasses of luminous wine frosty in the heat. Tuesdays are when people like me work. It's not a day to be away from your desk. Not a day to be asked to kill somebody. I'm trying to think. I can't. The mental indigestion is nice, in a way. It provides no outcome. Kloof Street is longer when you walk it. It gets steeper towards the top. It's different when you run. When you run you actually want the steepness and the hurt. Walking because you have to is just plain tedious. I pass the laundrette. Forty-nine steps further on, I remember that I'd dropped off a shitload of stuff on Saturday. I walk backwards down the hill. The hot bright world reverses its spin for a moment. I imagine walking backwards for the rest of my life. I imagine walking backwards for so long that I reverse through the years at the newspaper. Reverse through the drinking at Eric's and the shooting of the breeze with Madge. Reverse through the world to when Madge wasn't sick. Crazy maybe, not sick. I hit a lamppost just in time. Any more backwards-walking and I would have spun the world back to the Time Before. To scabs being picked open and covered holes undug. The bin attached to the lamppost catches me in a kidney. A flash of pain. Probably what Madge feels twenty-four seven. All over her body. I put Madge aside and go to the laundrette. Pay for my stuff. Walk home.

Mrs. du Toit darts into the lift just before the doors close. "Laundry?" she says. It's a red day. A repeat of the white day. Everything's red. Red tights, red sleeveless top. Red shoes. I wonder if she's shaved yet. The door shuts out the sunlight. It keeps in the brightness. The red of her outfit glows. It almost hurts to look at it. Her skin glows too, like candle wax with a flame behind it. I can smell the grease of the lift and something soft and floral and warm percolating through it from Mrs. du Toit's corner. She's an aromatherapy candle. Red and fragrant and glowing.

"Huh?" I say.

"Laundry?" she repeats, more slowly.

"Yup," I say.

"Ag," she says. "Come do it at my place next time. The tumble dryer works brilliantly." The porn movie continues. She laughs. I see fillings. Her laugh opens my mouth.

"How about a drink later?" I say. It just comes out. She can say yes or no. She doesn't have to throw her head back and show me her fillings again. The lift makes its lift noises. The door opens on our floor with a ping. I hold the button down so that she can get out. So that she can go and join her phantom husband in her flat and leave me alone.

"Okay," she says.

I SET THE alarm for five. I close my eyes and instantly can't sleep. It's not the light. I only ever sleep with a light on. No. There are twenty-four hours' worth of spreadsheets projected on my eyelids. The numbers dance and duck and dive. They make no sense and then they do and then they don't again. At one point I have a flash of doubt. I wonder if we should have approached the whole proposal differently. I fall asleep at about two. I'm going to shower and shave when I wake up. Put on some of the clean clothes from the laundrette. Splash on the cologne that Sonia gave me on my first anniversary at the paper. Take Mrs. du Toit to

Eric's. When the alarm goes I slap it repeatedly. I eventually get up at six. I do all those things I've promised myself. Shower, shave and so on. Knock on Mrs. du Toit's door. It's a black night. Black tights, black sleeveless top, black shoes. Her eyes are puffy.

"Sorry, I worked all night and overslept," I say.

"That's okay," she says. What I hear is, "Vat's okay."

We take a tuk-tuk to Eric's. I don't have a car. Cars are for people who want to go somewhere. I can't exactly ask Mrs. du Toit to drive. Eric looks at me funny when we walk in. I look around for Sonia. I'm thinking of what to say to her. Not that she's going to be here after last night. Nobody is here, in fact. Nobody important. Just one or two guys from the newsroom. There's a girl with them. She looks about fifteen. An intern, I suppose. The journos are trying to impress her. It's working. We find a booth away from the bar and the journos. Another first for me. We drink. We talk. I don't know what we talk about. All sorts of shit. It doesn't matter. It's just words. What they are isn't important. As long as they don't dig and probe. At some point she slips a foot out of a black shoe. The foot is on my shin, my calves. Then between my thighs. I can't remember if my socks have holes in them or not. I look up and there's nobody else in the pub. Eric is nodding towards the door. Mrs. du Toit and I have had a lot to drink. I tell her we should go.

Of course we end up fucking. Her bed is neatly made. There are posies of fresh flowers in little vases on either side of it. She knew this was going to happen. I hate it when people pre-empt you. She doesn't even know me. First she goes to the bathroom. She half-closes the door. I spy on her. I'm hoping she's going to pee. Instead she picks up a glass and swallows some pills. She's grinning when she comes back. Mrs. du Toit peels off her black clothes. Her legs are long and strong. Hourglass hips. I'm lying on the bed with all my clothes on. Even my shoes. I worry about the condition of my socks. Mrs. du Toit's goodies are hidden by black frills. She has a bit of a paunch. She takes off her bra. I see she's done her armpits. Once released, her breasts are enormous. She has areolas like dinner plates. There are little pet nipples dotted all around the real ones. As if she'd be happy to feed a school of remora fish or orphaned babies all at once. Finally she slips off her black panties. She has a great big fantastic arse straight out of a fifties' swimsuit calendar. Her fanny has a strip of hair down the middle. She probably shaved it herself. It leans to one side like an exclamation mark Bugs Bunny might use. "Yee-hah!" she shrieks. She launches herself at me. I'm still worried about my socks.

THERE IS NO alarm clock on the table beside Mrs. du Toit's bed. I reach for my phone. It is already eight. A slice of sunlight falls between the curtains. For a moment I don't know if it's Saturday or Sunday. It's Wednesday. I'm supposed to be at work by eight-thirty. My left arm is wedged under Mrs. du Toit's cheek. My pinkie and ring finger are both numb. Her mascara has gone awry again. It looks like she's been punched in the nose. It's so very beautiful. Her breath smells like night and booze and probably like my cock. I can't tell. I can't remember anything beyond her pouncing on me. Now Mrs. du Toit is smiling in her sleep. I suppose the downside of last night is that I won't hear her doing herself for a while. I move my arm and she makes a noise like a cat. I wriggle my arm out. She doesn't wake up. I have a morning erection. Of course I am tempted to sink it into her. While she is still asleep. Her one leg is drawn up almost to her chin. The other is stretched out behind her. It looks as if she's running. Or trying to jump over a ditch. Between them lies an easy target. Trusting and vulnerable. She smells like yesterday. I go to her bathroom and pee for ever. My hard-on disappears. I wonder how my clothes might look in her washing machine. Or in the dryer we sweated and stank to install. I pull on my jeans and sneak the short distance to my flat. Have a shower and wash the forty years of Mrs. du Toit off of me. Go to work to face Wednesday.

MY HEADACHE HAS almost gone by the time I get to the office. Sonia is being talked at by Dino. I'm sure he thinks I'm gay. I'm not. Been there, tried that.

I think.

Sonia doesn't see me sneak to my desk. Ally comes back to me with a few small changes. It's late afternoon when Sonia comes shrieking into my cubicle. She's brandishing the client signature on a scanned thing. She wants to go to Eric's to celebrate. I turn her down. Her eyes widen. I've never before noticed the white bits of her eyes around the blue. The deal makes up pretty much my entire target for the year. It's only February. "Don't clap, throw money," I say to her. I'm pissing her off. I'm trying to. I have more money than I need. It's piling up in a bank account. I don't know what the big thing is with money. I don't want to go to Eric's. The truth is I'm on to something more interesting at the moment. A great soft laughing thing. I don't care that Mrs. du Toit is ten or twelve years older than me.

IT'S THE THURSDAY after the Wednesday. There we are again. Me sockless, Mrs. du Toit skewly shaven, her areolae like twin rising moons. An empty bottle of faux champagne is on the bedside table. We're eating each other like lunch. Her belly slapping against me. It's the laughing I'm not used to. Maybe it's the pills. Are they meant to keep her laughing, I wonder. Or just on an even keel?

The next day Madge leaves a message on my phone. I am to be at her flat on Saturday afternoon. She gives the address. Mrs. du Toit notices my morning glory. I am late for work again.

I'VE NEVER BEEN to Madge's place. It's a flat in Gardens. The block smells of old burp. I'd imagined that she lived in a treasure chest of the kinds of things we used to buy on our trips. In a rambling mansion with paint peeling from the woodwork. Mossy flagstones and sunlight dull on dusty wooden floors. Mismatched candles askew in huge pewter candelabra on a table as long as runway. A big brindle dog dozing in the sun. She doesn't. Madge's flat is tiny and bare and smells like shit and medicine. It looks onto the branches of a dead tree. Behind it is a brown brick wall. Pipes come out of it.

"The details," Madge says.

It cannot be a suicide. That's what's been holding her back. She is Catholic. I didn't know this. For me religion is like a car accident. Fascinating to observe, horrifying to be involved in. Catholics don't bury suicides in consecrated ground. Suicides don't go to heaven. It sounds mediaeval. It can't be that hard to persuade them. Or God. It's 2014, for heaven's sake. Also, she has a life policy. It won't pay out on suicide.

Then she tells me her dodgy nephew is the beneficiary.

"Change it, Madge. There's time," I tell her. "What's he

ever done for you? Where has he been for the last four or five years? Fuck him."

Madge stares at me. "Oh, so *you* want it?" she says. She's being an uncharacteristic bitch to me. I can see she knows that. I don't think she can help herself.

"He's an arsehole, Madge. You've told me so yourself. Two months and it'll all be gone." On casinos and cheap crack. Alcohol and whores.

"That will be two months after I've gone," she says. "So double you tee eff." She spits out the acronym. Then she softens. "Anyway, what would you do with it?"

I look at her hard.

"If it were yours, I mean. If you were in my situation."

"Give it to a kennel or to people who feed African kids."

"We *are* in Africa. He *is* an African kid. You make it sound like they all live in Niger or Malawi."

"I meant poor kids, small ones, if that clarifies. There are starving, raped, abandoned AIDS kids right here. There are kids down the road who can't go to school. So kids who've pissed away every opportunity shouldn't qualify."

"Hah," she says. It's what she always says when she's lost an argument. She stares at the pipes growing from the wall outside. I've never seen her sadder. "It's not just the nephew and the life policy. It's not just the Catholics. It's sixty or so years' of life, Nate." There's the dead husband, she says, who watches over her all the time. It's the friends she's accumulated over decades. She will categorically not attract any guilty sympathy. And there's history too, she says. The sixties. The seventies. Psychedelia. The tentacles of Haight-Ashbury reaching even here. Creeping in under the Calvinist conservatism of 1970s South Africa. Sharing drugs. Spreading legs. Breaking hearts. The ones who survived are old friends now. There is pride, she tells me. Pride precludes pity and knowing looks.

"Pride?" I say. I'm trying to imagine her friends. I can't.

"I don't have much else. And it's getting harder by the day to hang onto it." She stands up, rummages in a cupboard. She pulls out a bottle of Johnnie Black. Its shoulders are covered with dust. Whisky doesn't go off. She tries to twist the top. Gives up. Hands me the bottle.

"Single or double?" I ask.

"Neither," she says. "That would be the worst. I haven't been able to drink for eighteen months."

I pour her a lime and soda. I pour myself a triple. I add another finger. I knock some back, top it up again. There's no ice. The whisky burns in my throat. I sit on the orange couch. Madge sits on a stiff-backed wooden thing. It looks Victorian. I'm sure it has a little knob carved into the back so that you can't slouch.

"What's next?" Madge says.

Again she's lost me.

"A hospice where they'll clean up after me as I expel ever more from my various orifices. Doctors I don't know and nurses who don't care. Tests and more tests. Drugs and more drugs. Pointless and vain. Like Canute, stopping nothing, least of all the pain. And then it finally ends with a whimper. Do you know that the last orifices are within the skin itself, that your fluids leak through your pores at the end?"

She sips her lime and soda. I can see she isn't enjoying it. Then she smiles. "I want to go with a bang. Not much of a bang, just a bit of a one. I can't go trickling to a stop. I *won't*, you know."

I swirl my Johnnie around in the glass. Even though there's nothing to mix it with. Madge watches the bubbles rising through her drink. She perks up.

"You can have my shop." She sings the words. It's like she doesn't mean them. "You do me and the shop is yours," she says.

I understand now. The understanding makes me knock back my whisky. "Fuck you, Madge," I say. My tongue is behind my teeth, ready to strike. I could sting her like an asp. I don't want her *anything*. What I want is for her not to die.

"No, fuck *you*," she says.

"Fuck me?" I try to sound indignant. What I hear is, "Fugg me." Okay, so the whisky has my tongue. It has other parts of me too. The parts in the middle of me. The parts around my lungs and my heart. It hurts. It makes me want to sob. I do. Snot shoots out of my nose. Madge takes the tissue from under her strap. I take it. "I don't want your policies or your shops. I don't want to kill you either," I say.

"Come, Nate," she says. "It's not that hard to understand. I'm dying and I'm not. I'm trying and I can't. Every day is a living death, and that thing called life is as far from me as Steve McQueen is from you. And like old Steve, I'll never see the real thing again."

Every breath catches and chokes so that I can't speak. I last cried like this when I was a kid. Madge's tissue isn't enough. I'm using my wrists, my sleeves. She watches me and waits. She levers herself out of her chair. She takes my glass. She pours twice what I'd poured earlier. Shoves it towards me. I gulp. It hurts. Halfway through I have a huge hiccup.

"Murder me, darling," Madge says. "Please."

I SLEEP ON HER ORANGE COUCH

I sleep on her orange couch in my clothes. I wake up at dawn. As usual I have a hard-on. Half of it I put down to a full bladder, and half to being indefatigably horny. It's up against my jeans on the left. It hurts. There's a small toilet next to Madge's lounge. While I'm peeing, I wonder at the silence. I wonder if I killed her in the night. I can't remember anything beyond whisky and crying and sounding petulant. My body breaks out in goose bumps. It's not a cold day. My knees turn to balloons of water. I put my hand up to the wall so that I don't pee all over the cistern. My prostate has a little fit of its own. I pee in spurts. Like an ornamental fountain. So much pee and so little time. Did I use a kitchen knife? Did I find a hammer somewhere? Or did I smother her with an orange cushion? When I've finished peeing I look at my hands. Squint at the places where blood might collect. Under the finger-nails. In the cuticles. I see nothing. I wash my hands just in case. Scrub them with Madge's nailbrush. Stare at the basin for a while. Wonder about luminol. Other forensic stuff they probably have and never show on TV.

The door to Madge's bedroom is open just a crack. I

nudge it, waiting for the horror-movie creak. There isn't one. I can't go in. I have to. I can't see in the murk. I stand in the doorway, waiting for my eyes to adjust. A glow filters through the blinds. I make out a shape on the bed. A silvery strand of drool dangles from the corner of her mouth. It dips in the hollow of her cheek and stretches like a spiderweb to her earlobe. In the middle of the lobe is a tiny diamond stud. It's an old person's earlobe, long and soft. Madge inhales, emits a gentle snort. Even in her sleep she hugs her sides. Evidently I didn't kill her. I leave a note. *See you later—N*, I write.

So banal.

It almost undoes last night's conversation all by itself. I like banal. It's why I work where I work. It's why I live where I live. Why I live how I live. I'm not Dino.

I TAKE THE STAIRS IN CASE

I take the stairs in case Mrs. du Toit is lurking in the lift. I don't feel like her right now. At the top I peer around the corner. I don't see her. Maybe she's gone to church. Maybe not. The open passageway has a brick balustrade along its length. You have to walk past doorways and the windows of kitchens and bathrooms. You can see the saddle between Lion's Head and Signal Hill. In winter when it rains you can be totally drenched on the way to your door.

My door clicks open and still she doesn't appear. I pull it shut. Lock it. Slowly slide the chain into its slot. I take the old photographs down from the wall. I'm always careful how I put them up. I use thin red ribbon to connect one to the next. I'm just as careful when I take them down. It's silent behind the wall. Once I've removed the photographs, the strips of ribbon make up a giant family tree that's lost its leaves. I don't take down the last two images. One is a photo of me. I'm twelve years and three months old. I don't remember how I know. I just do. I'm standing in dappled shade. There is a lake behind me. There are pine trees to my left and right. I'm not very big in the picture. There's shadow over my face and sunlight on the top of my hair. It was lighter then. Short. Shiny. It's hard to see *me* in the picture. The other picture is of my sister. Isabel about eight in the photograph. Hair like a helmet. It wasn't taken at the same time as mine. She'd have been eighteen or so on the day my picture was taken. Almost forty today. I wonder what she looks like now. I wonder if she also wears single colours like Mrs. du Toit.

I take the strips of ribbon from the wall. I drape them carefully over the back of a chair. I take the photograph of the woman at the airfield and stick it above my sister and me. I use three bits of ribbon to connect our pictures to hers. One piece goes across from me to my sister. Then a shorter bit connects us vertically to the airfield woman. She's our mother now.

I open the album and pop each photograph from its triangular mount. I should be wearing white gloves for this. Like they do in museums. I line up the photographs on the coffee table. They're in the same order as they were in the album. It's sort of sad to see them laid out one after another. The whole thing takes me hours. Like always. I stand up, find some bread. Wash it down with Sparberry. Get back to work.

There's a knock on my door. My knee hits the coffee table. I've been concentrating hard in the silence. I hope I haven't made a noise. It's getting dark. I need to switch on a light.

"Nathan?" Mrs. du Toit coos. "Naa-than." I freeze. If I move the couch springs will squeak. She knocks again. Calls my name. I can hear her breath at the door. Huffing and puffing, wanting to blow my house in. I hope she doesn't hear my breathing. My shin hurts. If I didn't know who it was I would be afraid. I don't get visitors. Then I hear high heels clicking. Red or white or black heels. Keys being fiddled with. It takes her a while to open her door. She slams it, almost. I hear her locks being locked and her chains being chained.

It takes me past midnight to build my new family. The first step is to edit out the ones that don't fit your story. Then you have to figure out the connections between all the rest. You make mistakes and start again. You carry on editing. Sometimes you rescue a discarded face from the slush pile. Sometimes you select a face and then reject it later. You constantly ask yourself, "What if?" It makes you think. It helps you build the stories and the backstories. It helps you be sure that everything is logical and tight.

I fall asleep on the couch.

I wake up and know I've had The Dream. I hardly ever dream. When I do it's always the same one. My neck is stiff. The dream has no pictures. It's just black. It smells of pine needles. In the blackness is the sound of someone crying. There's also the smell of something mouldy. My heart is thumping as if I've been running up the mountain.

It's always like this when I wake up from The Dream. I look at my wall of photographs until I'm calm again. I need a run. It's two am. I go to bed. Set my alarm for six.

I RUN INTO the wind. It's strong. It's beatable. It's a barrier of marshmallow. The marshmallow smells like sun and dust and fynbos. I run all the way along Tafelberg Road. I turn around at the ravine near Devil's Peak. There's a barrier there now. It's been put there to block cars from going any further. A sign warns of rockfalls. Just beyond is an old reservoir at a bend in the road. The water in it is black. There are frogs. The wind is at my back on the way home. I'm pushed along by a giant marshmallow that smells of mountain.

When I get out of the lift I hear my cellphone ringing in my flat. I don't get the door open in time. I see a missed call from Mrs. du Toit. I call her back. I can hear her phone ringing through the wall. It's playing "The Sting." One ear hears her voice next door. The other hears her voice on my phone.

"Come for breakfast," she says. "And bring your laundry."

"I've just come back from a run. I need to shower and get to work."

I'm looking at my family on the wall as I speak. There is a picture of a woman who irritates me. She is in profile. She has a heavy jaw. Her braided hair sits on top of her head. On top of the braids is a small floppy hat. Maybe it's a handkerchief. The white of her blouse fades into the white of the background. She has a smile. A grin. It's almost too modern, that smile. Candid and toothy. Perhaps that's what's irritating me. I'll get rid of her sometime.

"Come shower here," Mrs. du Toit says.

I'm not wearing a shirt. I am dripping sweat. The phone feels slippery in my hand.

"I have to be at work by eight-thirty," I say.

"Have to? Says who?"

There's a silence.

"Okay," I say. I text Sonia to tell her I'm sick. She hates it when staff text like that. She expects them to call. She wants to hear the sickness in their voices. She's been known to go to their homes if she doesn't believe them. I turn off my phone. I kick off my running shoes. Pull off my socks. They have holes in them.

I knock on Mrs. du Toit's door. I have a bundle of smelly clothing in my arms. I drop a sock and pick it up. Mrs. du Toit is wearing a white towel. She knew things would happen like this. She's planned for it. Again. The towel is tied over her breasts in that secret woman-knot that stops it sliding off. It's tied high, so it's short. The thrust of her breasts makes it even shorter in front. The high heels are a bit much. Mrs. du Toit grabs my arm and pulls me into the flat. She's giggling. She makes a show of peeping out of the door before she closes it. Pretending to make sure that nobody has been watching. She isn't a good actor. There's a cheap coffee filter machine on the counter. It's making noises and dripping brown liquid into a glass pot. The room smells of coffee. Mrs. du Toit drags me to the bathroom. She takes my clothes. She squats at the washing machine and stuffs them in through the glass door. Whites, colours, blacks all together. I don't mind. I don't care how they come out. As long as they're clean.

She curls a forefinger at me. "Come," she says. I step closer. She laughs. "Your shorts," she says. I step out of them. "And?" she says. She holds out her hand for my underpants. I take them off. There is a great dark sweat stain down the back of them. She throws them in with the rest of the laundry. She stands and turns the machine on. Then she turns to me and cocks her head to one side. Her smile is a caricature of someone being sexy in the movies. She puts out a finger and runs it down my chest. She puts the tip of it into her mouth. Then she undoes the towel. It drops to the floor. She steps up to me and takes my balls in one hand. She sticks her tongue down my throat.

Having sex in the shower isn't easy. It only really works in books and movies. We stop trying and head for the bed. Soon the bed is as wet as we are. She pours coffee afterwards. Sips it as she scrambles some eggs. Piles this onto toast. We are naked. We eat breakfast naked. I wash the dishes naked. I hear the washing machine change cycles. She laughs and flashes fillings.

"You're stuck," she says. She nods towards the noise. "No clothes." She leads me to the bedroom by my dick.

I COULD EASILY DO EVERY MONDAY

I could easily do every Monday like this. I could easily not work for a living. The trouble with bunking Monday is that it makes Tuesday much worse. The hangover of all that unfinished Monday business. The more of Monday we use up, the closer Tuesday is. Mrs. du Toit isn't that bad, I decide. She falls asleep next to me. She's almost beautiful. I watch her as the day ticks away. When we wake up we shake out my clothes. I put some on. We go out for a late lunch. A burger at the place on the corner of Kloof Street. It's not very good. We only drink one bottle of wine between us. She chats. A lot. I don't mind. The more she talks about herself the less she can ask about me. She starts to go on about her husband. She goes quiet and stops talking. I suddenly want to tell her all about Madge. About what Madge wants. I swallow the words down. Either the stories about herself or the wine has made her sad.

"Come," she says. I can see she's trying to shake it off. "Let's walk." I like to run. I hate walking. We go to the Company's Garden. It used to be a vegetable garden for sailors. There are ponds. There are homeless people.

Bronzes of old jingoists. Rhodes. Smuts. General Somebody on a horse. Mrs. du Toit is wearing jeans and sneakers. It's almost dark. At Wale Street we turn back and head up to Gardens again. A last peanut vendor is trying to offload his day's stock. He thinks we're tourists. He tries to sell us a bag of peanuts to feed to the squirrels. "No thanks," Mrs. du Toit says in Afrikaans. She holds on to my arm with both hands. It's like she's trying to crawl into me. I know she'll take it badly if I shrug her off. There aren't many people left in the avenue. We're halfway back when Mrs. du Toit stops. I look at her. She holds a finger to her lips. I listen. A bush is snoring. A pair of tattered sneakers protrudes from it. I wonder whether Mrs. du Toit is going to laugh. She shakes her head. She isn't laughing. I suppose the feet of a homeless man sticking out of a bush is only funny if you're twelve.

At my door she stops. I am a little disappointed. She kisses me on my cheek. Pats the spot she's kissed. Goes to her flat.

SONIA HAS HELD over our Monday meeting to Tuesday because of my Monday illness. Yumna is on time. Already everyone has heard about Sarel's ARs comment. Now they're all calling him Arse. Sonia tells everyone about my big sale. They already know of course. They congratulate me. The make jokes about "the bank job" and "the heist."

I laugh when they laugh. I can taste the envy behind their words.

I don't feel like working. I try to remember my Monday with Mrs. du Toit. It's patchy. I go into Sonia's cubicle with my coffee. It looks like she does feel like working. She's spreadsheeting away. Every time I open my mouth to say something she makes a phone call or holds her hand up. At the edge of her desk is a reporter's notepad. It's spiral-bound with a blue line down the middle. I pick it up. The inside cover has Dino's name and cellphone number on it. The first eight or ten pages are covered with shorthand scrawl. I can't make out a thing. I wonder whether there are murder or corruption or hijacking syndicates hidden in the cyphers. The thought of big macho Dino making notes in old-fashioned secretary's script makes me smile. Sonia is boring me. I take the notepad to my desk. I tear off Dino's notes. I ball them up. I wrap the ball in another sheet of paper. I drop it into the bin. I slip the notepad into the pocket of my hoodie. I have a plan for it. I just don't know what it is just yet. Sometimes plans only reveal themselves once you have all the bits to hand.

By four-thirty Sonia is also bored. We pretend we have a meeting upstairs. We take the lift to the ground floor. Eric drops his pen and starts pouring our drinks as we walk in. Beers for both of us. I like women who like beer. The bar is quiet. Eric resumes his drawing. It's of some elf or sprite or troll or something. Above the waist it splits into two creatures. They're fighting with each other.

"So," Sonia says. It's the kind of "so" that's heavy with what's to come. She raises her glass at me. "Well done on the bank thing," she says. So, that wasn't the reason for the "so." It must be about my Monday sickness. I wait for it.

"Thanks for your help," is what I say and toast her back.

She shrugs. "That's what I'm there for." She drinks her beer. "You need to know that it's been noticed by bigger people than me," she says. "One or two more like that during the year and you might have my job soon. You just need a bit of focus. Being on time. And not pulling sickies for no good reason."

"Two things," I say. "One, the bank thing was pure fluke. Ally could have called anyone. You. Sarel. Yumna. I didn't actually *do* anything to land it. And two, I really don't want your job."

"Gee, thanks." She frowns into her beer. "It's not such a bad job, by the way."

"It's not that. I'm happy where I am. How I am."

Sonia looks at me hard. Her little eyes grow littler. I wonder whether she can actually see me out of the slits. "How old are you?" she asks.

The enigma of these women.

"Thirty-one," I say.

"Do you have absolutely no ambition?"

I pretend to think about this for a moment. I'm wondering why this should be surprising.

"Nope," I say.

"So you don't want to be rich? Famous?"

"Nope."

"Just famous?"

"Definitely not."

"Just rich, then?"

I shrug. "I could do rich if I didn't have to work for it," I say.

"Not going to happen."

I don't see what's so hard to understand. "Listen. I don't want my name on a door. I don't want it in the movie credits. There are more people alive today than have ever died. Did you know that? Seven billion. How many of the dead ones do you remember? Ten? Twenty? How many of the alive ones can you name? The one billion that have roofs over their heads and enough to eat are climbing over each other to be on top of the pile before they die. The ones with the most toys win, remember? They say that after people were gassed by the Nazis, the camp officials would find them in a pyramid. The ones that died first were at the bottom. The toughest climbed to the top because they thought they could get to fresh air and survive."

"That's just gross," Sonia says.

"And guess what? The ones who made it to the top

of the pyramid ended up just as dead as the ones at the bottom." I stop. I'm losing track here.

"And your point is?"

I remember my point. "That however hard you work, however smart you are, however cut-throat or greedy or tough or whatever, you're going to end up just as dead as the Somali baby or the Iraqi car-bomb victim or the Jew at the bottom of the gas-chamber pile. I'm happy to be one of the seven billion. The alive seven billion. The little ones. The ones whose names you can't remember or will never know. The ones who go through life and then just kind of dissolve away at the end of it. I couldn't be arsed to sweat blood so that I can sit on more cash than the Pope and bequeath hospitals and establish foundations or give every third-world kid an iPad." I have a drink of beer. "I'm happy to sell ad space and grow old and sick and slip off the old mortal coil with no fanfare or monuments." I'm thinking Madge here. I had pulled a curtain across our Saturday discussion. It's slipping open again.

"Wow. That's quite a sermon."

"No it's not. Sermons need God."

"Huh?"

"Never mind," I say.

Sonia is frowning. She scratches her head. Her hand disappears up to the wrist in her bush of hair.

"The ultimate point—the point of all points—is that I have satellite TV. I'm happy the way I am."

"Are you? Really?" she says. "Just think. Money buys you things that do things for you. Money buys you idyllic holidays. Money buys you mansions with a view of the ocean. Money buys you designer labels and sports cars and enormous big flatscreen TVs. Money buys you freedom. Money buys you people who clean your house and do your washing."

"I already have someone who does my washing," I say.

IT'S A QUIET WEEK

It's a quiet week at work. I will it to be even quieter. I wish it wasn't quite so quiet on the fourth floor of Pansyshell Park, Tamboerskloof. Mrs. du Toit has vanished. Or else she's bunkered down and doesn't want to see me. I'm avoiding Madge. The notebook I've stolen is for her. If there's one thing I've learned from Mrs. du Toit, it's how to plan. When I speak to Madge again, it will be about planning. Wednesday is the worst. Nobody wants to go out for a drink after work. The inertia is not just mine. It's like a thick wet blanket over everyone. I go to Eric's on my own and watch him draw the same old alpine scene while we discuss the heat. It's a silly conversation. Sometimes words are easier than silence. Eric has cranked up his air con to arctic levels. I go home.

I close my door and hear Mrs. du Toit through my family-tree wall. She hasn't been in the lift or stalking my doorway for days. The woman with the jaw like a boxer's is still irritating me. I am a little jealous of Mrs. du Toit's self-jollification. I consider interrupting her. It's hard not to once I've had my ear to the wall. The buzzing and the moaning. I wish she'd put in a load of washing. From this angle the woman at the airfield looks a lot like Mrs. du Toit.

I call her at seven in the morning.

"What's for breakfast?" I ask. "I'm cooking." In your flat, I don't say.

She opens the door to me and she's dressed for the day. I'm disappointed. I'm relieved that I have my working clothes on. She gives me a hug. It's chaste. Like a Sonia hug.

"No cooking, just toast and coffee," she says.

I put bread in the toaster. Load up her crap coffee machine. Ask her casually if she's been busy. Add, coyly, that I've missed her. It isn't an absolute lie.

She tells me she'd spent a few days with her sister in Stellenbosch. The sister married well. The wine farm is doing even better. We eat the toast. I've burnt it a little. The coffee is passable.

"Let's do sushi tonight," I say.

"Raw fish?" she shrieks. She throws her head back and her fillings glint. "Okay."

So just when I thought things had gone south, Mrs. du Toit and I are sharing dishes at an Asian place in Church Street. I like it here because there won't be anyone from the paper poncing about. The prices on the menu confirm that. Mrs. du Toit shovels dim sum and prawns and sashimi. She does a Thai curry and asks for crab. Once she's hoovered everything in my budget I ask her if she'd like dessert.

"You," she leans forward, "are my dessert."

I'm not, actually. Something hasn't agreed with her. I hold her hair out of her face while she vomits. I help her to her bed. I brush the splatters off the toilet bowl. I help her to the toilet. I hold her hair. I brush the splatters. I consider taking her from behind while she's hunched over the toilet bowl. I don't.

I spend the night with her. In the morning she looks at me and says, "Christ." She runs to bathroom. I make her black tea. I go to work.

I HAVE TO SPEAK

I have to speak to Madge. I'm sure Dino's blank notebook holds the secret. If Mrs. du Toit can plan things for me, Madge and I can plan things for ourselves too. A notebook would help. It's Friday so everyone wants to sneak out early and go to Eric's after work. I tell them I'll see them there. I have some work to finish before the end of the day. It's a lie. I expect Sonia to raise an eyebrow. She doesn't. I go to Madge's shop. Today's dress is pale green and shiny. The scarf is a deep pink silk. Crimson, she would probably call it. Pink and green sound like they shouldn't go together. They do.

"Conditions," I say to Madge. "I won't get arrested. Ever." I think for a moment. "That's the only one."

"The perfect murder," Madge says.

"And no mess. I can't do mess. That's another."

Madge nods. "Two conditions, then," she says.

I pull Dino's notebook from the pocket of my hoodie. "We need to plan this," I say. "Meticulously."

"Meticulously," says Madge. "Surely our planning will go better with a cup of tea." There's no milk. I go around the corner up Church Street to the kiosk on Burg. I make sure the Somali hasn't slipped me expired milk. Like he did last time.

I make tea. Decline a biscuit. We begin. Guns are not an option. We wouldn't know where to get one. Or how to use the thing. We could make it look like an accident. An overdose of the medication she's refused to take. Electrocution. A short circuit in the shop. The kettle, perhaps. Or an electrical fire. She doesn't want to burn. Doesn't want to endanger anyone else. I tell her she could have a penicillin reaction to the mouldy biscuits in her cupboard. We laugh. What if someone broke into her flat, I venture. "Then they'd have to rape me," she says, "so that's not going to happen." A car accident, I say. We could disconnect her brakes. Messy, she says. Complicated. Unreliable. I make another pot of tea. It still doesn't leak from the cracks in my cup. We come up with ever more ludicrous ideas. We laugh. There are a few doodles on Dino's pad.

"We're not very good at this, are we now?" says Madge. She stares at the stuff in her shop. Her smile fades. The fading reminds me that this isn't a parlour game. We've wasted the last hour.

A man in a suit wanders up to the shop. He hesitates in the doorway and looks at his watch. It's well past five. Madge has forgotten to lock up. The man has a thick black moustache. The eyebrows look like its offspring. He has a thick nose and glasses with frames that are black and heavy. For a moment I wonder if he's wearing one of those off-the-shelf Groucho Marx disguises.

"Are you still open?" he asks.

"Seem to be," Madge says.

Groucho pokes around. Fingers a whole lot of stuff. Picks things up and puts them down. He brings a small bronze Beethoven bust to the counter. He raises his eyebrows. "How much is this?"

Why would you want to buy a crappy bust of Beethoven at five-thirty on a Friday evening, I wonder. Someone else comes in. Madge sees him and rolls her eyes. The new guy is young. He's wearing a hoodie. He is amazingly skinny. Meth, I think. He looks nervous. Something clicks into place in my brain.

"That's two thousand five hundred and forty," I say to Groucho. The little bust is mass-produced. One among a million souvenirs from Bonn or Vienna or wherever.

He turns it over. Under its base is a price tag. "It says seventy-five," he says.

"Three thousand seven hundred and seventy-five," I say. "Or get the fuck out of my shop."

He puts it down. Scurries out. Madge looks at me as if I've gone mad. I have. I'm watching myself from four, five, ten storeys up. I have X-ray vision. I can see through the bricks and the mortar. The kid in the hoodie has a soapstone sculpture of a tortoise in his hand.

"Two fifty-five," Madge sings. The kid looks at the thing he's holding.

"Too much," he says. "Thanks, anyway."

"You can have it for a hundred," I say. "Seventy-five if you buy something else as well."

Madge glares at me.

Christ, I want to say, you're dying. Let the man buy the tortoise. I've never tended customers in Madge's shop before. There's a first time for everything..

"Really?" the kid says.

"It's Friday," I say. As if that explains everything.

"Okay, then maybe I'll look around," he says.

"Help yourself," I say. "Take your time." The kid browses. He picks stuff up and puts it down.

"Seventy-five?" Madge hisses. "Seventy fucking five?" She's furious.

"It's a tortoise from Zimbabwe," I say. "It's not Degas's *Little Dancer*. The world does not rest on a tortoise." She has no idea what I'm talking about. I watch the kid. He fishes around. "I'll be back in a sec," I whisper to Madge. I go past the kid. Out of the shop. I can feel Madge's eyes on my back. I look up at the sky above St. George's Mall. I avoid looking directly at any of the security cameras. In Church Street I'm out of their view. I run. Unlock the gate to the alleyway. Madge's back door too. A plan is happening in my head. I feel like I'm having my out-of-body experience again. Like I'm floating fifteen metres in the air and watching me. My heart rate has gone ballistic. My mind is whirring like the cogs of the world's most complicated clock.

"Goodness," Madge says when I appear through the back door. I stay in the little corridor that is Madge's kitchen. I put a finger to my lips. She frowns. She's not getting it. Not at all. I'm relieved that the kid is still there. I need him for my plan. He picks things up and puts them down. He picks up other things and puts them down. I want him to take his time. I want him to hurry up. I slip Dino's pad into my pocket. It was useless for coming up with plans.

The kid takes the tortoise to the counter. "I'll just take this. A hundred is fine," he says.

Madge flicks a look at me. I worry that the kid will see me. He doesn't. He pays and goes.

"Where the hell did you go?" Madge asks. She's left the cash register open to cash up the few rand she's made for the day. I see a few dirty notes in the compartments.

"To the ends of the earth," I say.

She stands staring at me.

I go up to her and take the tails of her scarf in each hand. "Bye, Madge," I say. I begin to strangle her with the scarf. Her eyes bulge. She tries to shake her head. No, no, no, the shaking says. No no no! Too late now, Madge. It's harder than I'd thought. It takes a long time for her body to go limp. I let it slide to the floor. Her eyes are still open. I take the scarf and stuff it into my pocket with Dino's notebook. I have a hard-on. It's the craziest hard-on I've ever had. I've never come in my pants. I'm not far off. It's all I can do not to whip it out and do myself right there.

I run a quick inventory in my head. One, two, three things. I take all the notes from the register. Leave the change. I make sure again that I have the notepad and Madge's scarf. I take two squares of paper towel from the roll in the kitchen. Madge is still staring. She is lying behind the counter. Her head has flopped sideways. Her tongue protrudes from her mouth, blunt as a sausage. Thick and white and already dry. She would hate to see herself like this. Looking like a gargoyle. I can't help her.

"I love you, Madge," I say. I kiss her cheek. Everything I'm about to leave behind has a right to be there. My DNA on her face from a kiss. On a cracked china teacup. My fingerprints all over the place.

I go out through the back. I wipe the handle and the lock of the door with a square of paper towel. At the gateway to the alley I pretend to struggle with the lock and the bolt. It gives me a moment to wipe both of them with the other square. I still have a hard-on. Meth Boy is going to get it. I imagine him trying to convince the cops that he paid a hundred rand for a piece of soapstone. It's not going to work. My hard-on lasts all the way to Eric's. It hurts to walk. I wave at Sonia. She turns to order me a beer. I go straight to the gents. I sort out my hard-on. I flush the bits of paper towel away with everything else.

I FEEL TERRIBLE

I feel terrible in the morning. I go for a run anyway. I throw up in someone's driveway before I get to the top of Kloof Nek. I turn back. A newspaper poster on a street pole. *City Antique Dealer Murdered*. I bet Dino's name is all over the thing. I don't know if I puked because of the hangover. Or because of what I did to Madge.

I find a note in my bed. It's from Mrs. du Toit. It has an unsticky piece of Sellotape attached to it. *Came by, you not here*, it says. *Come to me when you get in—A*. It could have been stuck on my door last night. I don't remember. I shower. There's a pile of dirty clothing in my bath. I transfer Madge's scarf from the pocket of my jeans to my shorts. I pour a glass of Coke and stir it with a fork to get the bubbles out. I eat some dry toast. I feel a little better. There's a precipitous decline from the Edwardians to the Woman in Red. It should irritate me. It doesn't. I try not to look at the smiling woman with the big jaw. I collect the clothing from my bed.

"Big night?" Mrs. du Toit asks as she opens the door. She's trying to tease. I can see she's put out. I shrug. She flicks the tiniest frown at my bundle of washing.

"Work thing," I say. "We were celebrating a big sale."

"Okay," she says. Mrs. du Toit is wearing a summer dress. It's yellow. So are her shoes. Her face is made up. I can't see the pores in her skin.

"Were you on your way out?"

"It can wait," she says. She takes the clothing from me. In the bathroom she sees to the load with brisk movements. Maybe the laundry service is by invitation only. The yellow dress stays on. There are little crescents of sweat at her armpits.

"Come with me," she says. I follow her to the living room. I stop. She continues to the front door. "No, come with me to town. I've got a few things to do. Then we can go for coffee or something." She narrows her eyes. "Or are you embarrassed to be seen in public with an old woman like me?"

I am. I can't admit it to her. "Of course not," I say. It's not just that. I don't want to go. Or maybe I do. I don't actually give a shit either way. I'm trying not to think about Madge. I tell myself that she's in a better place now. I don't know what that place is. Maybe it's a worse place. There probably isn't either of those places anyway. My head hurts. I don't know.

We go in Mrs. du Toit's Golf. It's new. It smells of leather and chemicals. The fumes are probably giving us both cancer as we sit there. I expect her to drive with her seat pushed forward. With her nose almost on the wheel. She doesn't. From somewhere she takes a pair of sunglasses. Wraparounds. Retro-chic and probably expensive. "Seatbelt," she says. She sits back. She kicks off her yellow shoes and dumps them at my feet. She drives as if the car was an extension of herself. It's a fast car.

We go to Gardens Centre. It's a great ugly grey tower block of apartments built above a shopping mall. We go to the supermarket. We go to the German deli. She browses briefly through a clothing store and buys nothing. I'm pushing her trolley. I'm three steps behind her. She goes into the pharmacy. She takes a piece of paper from her handbag. She hands it to the woman behind the counter. The woman makes a fuss of getting a few boxes of pills together. It's not very exciting. She puts three boxes on the counter. Mrs. du Toit scoops them into her handbag before I can read the labels. We go to her car and pack her shopping into the boot of her Golf. There's a smell of pine needles from the bags. I push the empty trolley away. I turn back to the car. She's walking off.

"Come," she says. She hardly looks around.

I tag along. Like a little boy forced to go to the shops with his mother. We walk under the highway bridge. I can smell urine and old sweat. I'm trying to walk next to Mrs. du Toit. The pavement is too narrow. I follow behind. I'm looking at my little-boy feet. Then there's a policeman in front of me. Standing still and scowling. I want to fling my arms around him. Yes yes yes, it was me, I want to say, me who strangled Madge with her own pink scarf. No no no, I want to say, you've got the wrong guy. The policeman is carrying a KFC bag stuffed to bursting. He's pissed off because I almost walked into him.

A block down the road Mrs. du Toit turns into a side street. She walks into a place that was once a warehouse or a workshop. It smells of coffee. I look around at the coffee drinkers. I don't know anyone. We sit down. Mrs. du Toit takes off her sunglasses. She orders a mocha something and a glass of water. I order a flat white. I don't know what that is. I'm sure other people have ordered one before me. I'm sure it will be fine. Behind Mrs. du Toit sits a man with a laptop open on his table. He is sitting away from it. He has a newspaper in his hands. *City Antique Dealer Murdered*, the headline says. I'm sure Dino got a by-line. I can't see from here. Mrs. du Toit is talking. I don't know what she's saying. I nod and make noises now and then. I'm trying not to watch the man with the newspaper too hard. I wish he'd put the thing down and go back to his laptop. The waiter brings the coffee. Mrs. du Toit opens a box of pills without taking it from her handbag. She pops a couple out of a card. She swallows them with her water. Then she repeats the action with another box. She starts nattering again. The man puts down the newspaper and pulls his laptop closer. It's taken so long that I've almost finished my flat white. It's a lot better than the stuff from Mrs. du Toit's coffee machine.

I stand up and ask the man if I can borrow his paper for a minute. Mrs. du Toit is in mid-sentence. He hands me the scruffy bundle. Tells me to keep it.

Mrs. du Toit has gone quiet. She seems a little peeved. She picks up her coffee cup and looks away from me. Of course I know what the lead story is about. Dino has his by-line. The plan needs a few finishing touches now. I read for a moment. I let the newspaper fall. I put one hand to my mouth and then the other. The movement catches Mrs. du Toit's attention. Mrs. du Toit stops sulking. She puts down her cup and leans forward.

"What is it?" she asks. Her hand is on my forearm.

"Madge," I say. My voice is hoarse. And then I put on my crying face and my shoulders heave.

I'M SOBBING IN her car. I don't know why. I can't stop. It's like somebody else's face has been laid over mine. The face is crying without me and it won't let up. I have the hem of my T-shirt to my nose. I lower it. It's full of snot and tears. "I'm sorry," I say. In her flat she pulls the T-shirt off me. She puts me onto her bed. It's too hot to get under the covers. I'm still wearing my shorts. I can feel Madge's scarf in my pocket. Mrs. du Toit brings me a glass of water and two pills.

"They'll help," she says. "Trust me, I know."

I swallow them. I hear her leave the flat and come back with her shopping. There's rustling and clattering as she unpacks the bags. I lift an arm. It falls back onto the bed. My other arm is just as heavy. So are my legs. Madge has gone far away. The whole of me feels strange. It's not like beer. Or Madge's whisky. It's like I'm being played at an octave lower than normal. Like I've always been a violin and now I'm a cello. I try to lift my cello head. My neck has turned to jelly. If I'm so heavy why am I floating six inches off the bed, I wonder. Mrs. du Toit comes in. The yellow dress has a neon aura. She kicks off her shoes. Sits next to me.

"Better?" she asks.

I nod. I think I nod.

"Tell me about Madge," she says. Sonia knows about Madge. She knows that I used to visit her sometimes. That she was sick. It's pretty much all she knows about me I'm sure. Outside of work, at least. I tell Mrs. du Toit things that Sonia has never known. About our buying trips. How we loved confusing onlookers about our relationship. How we shared bedrooms at B&Bs. I tell Mrs. du Toit about the calm of tea in a cracked cup and stale biscuits. I tell her that Madge had absolutely no idea about antiques. I can't remember when last I told anyone so much. I'm not sure if I ever have. Mrs. du Toit says hardly anything. I stop talking. She probably thinks I've told her everything. Of course I haven't. She goes to the bathroom. I hear bathwater. She comes to the bedroom. She takes off her yellow dress. She takes off her underwear. I watch. I feel nothing. After her bath she climbs onto the bed. She curls up next to me and strokes my forehead. I think I fall asleep. I think I sleep all through Sunday. It doesn't matter.

It's just another day.

EVERYONE IS TALKING

Everyone is talking about the story Dino broke on the weekend. Madge Cartwright murdered not a hundred metres from the newspaper office. A botched robbery. An unlikely suspect arrested and released. Some old guy working at a city hotel. Another man has also been arrested. He is to be charged soon. I marvel at how Dino has managed to fill so many column-centimetres with so little.

Is it ironic that Madge was dying anyway? I try to remember the proper definition of irony. I can't. The news report is thin on detail.

"Why don't you go home," Sonia says. "You look like shit."

I tell her that I'll feel worse at home. "I'd rather go and speak to the cops," I say. "I was there on Friday afternoon. That's why I came to Eric's so late."

Sonia looks at me funny.

"For Christ's sake," I say. "We had tea. I left. There was a guy who couldn't decide what he wanted. I got bored." And then I ducked out and came back through the alleyway, I don't say. Waited for the boy to pay for his tortoise and leave. Strangled Madge with her scarf. This scarf right here in my pocket. What the security cameras would have seen is me leaving well before the boy. Looking up as if to check the weather.

I get the detective's name and number from Dino. I call Inspector Morris. I don't want him to come to the paper. I walk to Caledon Square. It takes the charge office half an hour to find him. I wait at the counter. The skin of my forearms sticks to its surface. The paint is peeling from the walls. Posters are peeling from the paint. The linoleum is peeling from the floor. People come and go. They all look small and furtive and broken. Or like they should be on the other side of the counter, in a holding cell. A young woman comes in. She explains that her car has been broken into. The constable behind the desk sighs. He bends down to get something from under the counter. A yellow folder. Some forms. A notepad. The young woman's face goes red. I need to pee. I'm worried that if I go to the bathroom I'll miss Inspector Morris. The constable starts asking the woman questions. He writes slowly. The pen looks uncomfortable in his hand. "No, I did not give anyone permission to break into my car," the woman shrieks. With each plosive, white flecks fly from her mouth. She is spitting all over the constable. "What the hell kind of a question is that?"

I am ushered into a room to meet Morris. I'm expecting a tough Cockney from a BBC cop show. I suppose it's the name. Morris has a heavy Afrikaans accent. It would be a mistake to associate the accent with stupidity. People have done that before. I'm not going to. The room is so small that he has to squeeze himself against the wall to get around the table. He sits opposite me. He thanks me for coming. I put my sad face on. I tell him the facts as I'd told them to Mrs. du Toit.

"So you've known the deceased for . . . ?"

"Four or five years," I tell him.

"And how did your friendship begin?"

"I work not too far from her shop," I tell him. "We talked about antiques. She was flamboyant and dramatic and interesting. She knew nothing about antiques." The personal note is a good touch. Tears come to my eyes. "I found it amusing. We started having tea together. I would go and see her after work. Even on a weekend sometimes."

"Forgive me, I have to ask. Was there anything, ah, inappropriate about your relationship?"

"Goodness, no." I sound just like Madge.

Morris wants to know about Friday. I tell him that I left work early and went to see her. That we chatted and had tea. That we were so preoccupied she forgot to close up at five. That a man came in to the shop just as I was leaving. That I was off to join some colleagues at a bar down the Mall. That I wanted to speak to police once I heard about the murder because my fingerprints would be all over the shop.

Morris nods. He makes notes on his yellow pad. He asks me to describe the customer. I describe Groucho Marx.

"He says you were exceptionally rude to him," Morris says.

I shrug. "He didn't want to pay the going price for an item."

"And?"

"And he left."

"Did someone else come into the shop at any point?"

"Yes. A young man. Scruffy, wearing a hoodie. Skinny as a junkie. The other customer might have noticed him before leaving."

"You left while the young man was in the shop?"

"Yes. I was late. It was more than just a drink with my friends. It was more like an after-work function. Informal. Still, you're expected to pitch. I couldn't wait any longer, so I left."

"You didn't feel that Miss Cartwright was at risk from this young man?"

"No. He seemed to be browsing like any other shopper. Anyway, he didn't exactly start shooting up in the shop."

Morris takes notes. I wonder how far to push my luck. I push.

"Do you think you have enough on him?" I ask.

Morris looks up. He is amused. I suppose it's my TV-programme language. "I can't divulge anything. Maybe there's something, maybe not. This police force isn't the one I joined thirty years ago, so who knows."

He stands up. Thanks me. I can't see his thoughts. He tells me to "be available." Tells me not to leave town. Laughs though his eyes don't. He calls a constable to take my fingerprints. She leads me to another room. She isn't very friendly. She has a long body and short legs. Or perhaps it's just the uniform. The jacket hanging over her hips. The knee-length skirt and flat shoes. The room is remarkable for its smears of ink everywhere. She inks the tips of my fingers. Then she takes each fingertip and rolls it onto a sheet of paper. There's a block for each finger. The ink is black and sticky. There's a stained basin in the room. She waves me towards it. The tiles behind the basin are cracked and chipped and spattered with ink. There's a plastic pot of petroleum jelly on the basin. I'm not sure what to do. The constable tells me to take some of the jelly and to clean my hands with it. I try this. The jelly smears the ink around my hands. There's a single sheet of paper in the dispenser. It doesn't help much. In seconds it's soaked and black. The constable opens a drawer and hands me a piece of newspaper. On it is the continuation of Dino's front-page story. The ink of the newspaper mixes with the ink on my hands.

BUGGER THE CUSTOMERS

"Bugger the customers," I mutter. I drop my handful of soil onto the lid of the coffin. I feel a look from the man next to me. It's Friday. Tuesday Wednesday Thursday smudged themselves together into one long forgettable day. Sonia has snuck me a day's compassionate leave. She said I should have taken more time off. Said I've been "different." There are lots of people at the funeral. Some are standing on their toes to see what's going on. I've counted them, more or less. I stopped at sixty. It's hot. I expected a handful. Six or seven acquaintances were what I'd imagined. Me the closest friend. I'm about the fortieth in line for the soil. I put my hand into my pocket and rub it clean on Madge's scarf. Everyone seems to have known her better than I ever did. I can't say how this makes me feel. They're muttering little anecdotes and recollections among themselves. I never hear my name. Nobody asks me how I knew Madge. The herd begins to shuffle away from the graveside. The mourners are a motley lot. None of them are smartly dressed. All sandals and scruffy jeans and seventies dresses. I suspect professors with out-of-fashion Marxist leanings. Poets and minor novelists. Other antique-store owners. I look for the weaselly nephew. I don't see him.

I consider skipping the wake. A true friend would attend. It's at the house of a certain Bevan and his wife Sienna. About half of the mourners arrive. The house is in the older part of Mowbray. An old car is parked under a fig tree. It's spattered with bird shit. Some of the shit calcified a long time ago. You wouldn't be able to see through the windscreen. Or clean it even. Loose tiles sit askew on the roof of the house. A gutter sags. It has grass sprouting from it. Paint is quietly peeling from the walls. Inside, the furniture is chipped and scratched. Crocheted throws and faded kikois cover couches and chairs. Hiding torn upholstery and broken springs, I'm sure. Someone hands me a plate of coleslaw. The plate is chipped. There are raisins in the gluey grey tangle. The raisins have absorbed the liquid. They're fat and black. Someone hands me a glass of white wine. It is warm and sour. I can't eat the coleslaw while I'm holding a glass of wine. I put the plate down. Someone fills my glass again. She is younger than the rest of them.

"Thanks. I'm Nathan, by the way," I tell her.

"Cindy," she says. She has two glasses in one hand. The wine bottle is in the other. I shake the finger she holds out to me. "How did you know Madge?" she asks.

"From the shop," I say.

"Oh, you're *that* Nathan," she says. "You were very kind to her towards the end." It's nice to get a mention. I hope Madge didn't mention too much. I leave without saying goodbye to anyone. I walk around Mowbray for ages. I finally find a taxi that will take me to town. I feel like a drink. It would be weird to go to Eric's. I'm supposed to be in mourning. I am, actually. I walk around until I find a bar. It's mostly full of bikers. No newspaper people. No Mrs. du Toit. Nobody I know at all. It's perfect. I order a beer.

I raise my glass to everything and nothing. Goodbye, Madge.

I KNOW MORE

"I know more about Madge than I do about you," says Mrs. du Toit. She was waiting for me after my Saturday morning run. Now we're eating ice cream on her bed. Ice cream pairs well with Merlot, she says. The more we drink the better it tastes. We've spent the morning doing things that can't be legal. I've never done anything like them. I'm worn out. The wine is making me tired. Even Sonia knows more about Madge than she does about me. I like it that way. Imagine standing in a big bucket. Every time you tell somebody something about yourself you're pouring a spadeful of concrete into the bucket. Soon enough it's up to your knees. It sets. You can't move.

"And you know more about Madge than I know about *you*," I say. She shrugs. I see the fear of the bucket cloud her eyes.

"I asked first," she says.

"Ladies first," I reply.

"Are you saying I'm a lady?" she laughs. She leans away from me and puts down her ice cream and her wineglass.

"Absolutely," I say.

"We'll see," she says. She lunges. I spill wine on her duvet.

Crisis averted.

I could tell Mrs. du Toit that I don't know much about me either. That I've chosen to forget as much as possible. If you think learning things is difficult, try forgetting them. Forgetting the Mandarin you've learnt to speak would be a lot harder than learning it in the first place. You can learn completely. You can never forget completely. The harder I've worked at it the easier the forgetting has become. Not very easy, just a little easier. Sometimes you think you've forgotten stuff. Then it catches you off-guard. While you're sleeping. When you're tired. Drunk. Madge with her dry white tongue sticking out between her teeth like that. A view of a lake. Darkness and the bitterness of pine needles. What goes with these. Then you hit a tipping point. Suddenly, the more you teach yourself to forget, the harder it becomes to remember. The forgetting invades the remembering. You start forgetting what you *want* to remember. Instead of just forgetting what you have to forget. Already I've forgotten the sound of Madge's laugh. I can't remember the taste of Mrs. du Toit for more than a few minutes after the deed.

She rolls off me. "Come," she says. Bounces off the bed and yanks my arm, "Let's go party."

I hate nightclubs. I don't dance very well. All those people. The thought of Mrs. du Toit in a red dress and red shoes in a nightclub. It doesn't appeal. "Come *on*," she says. She grabs the bottle of wine. She pulls me off the bed by my wrist. She puts on a CD. I don't know what it is. It's never going to be a classic. She slugs the rest of the wine from the bottle. She finds another bottle in a kitchen cupboard. She opens it. It has a screw-cap. She takes a long drink. She hands it to me. She starts dancing. It's grotesque. It's better than going out. I dance. I generally feel silly dancing. I feel even sillier with my cock flopping about. I drink more wine. I don't care. We finish the wine in less than half an hour. Mrs. du Toit looks for more. There isn't any. She sucks the last drops from the bottle. She puts it in the bin. She looks at me like she's had a brilliant idea.

"Let's have some pills," she shrieks.

The pills are big and pink in my hand. "What are these anyway?" I ask. She passes me her glass of water.

"Widow's little helpers," she says.

That's why there's no husband then. He's dead.

She laughs. We fall into bed. Nothing works. She laughs again and lies back. She splays her legs and throws out her arms. The back of a hand slaps me in the face. She laughs. Laugh laugh laugh, I think. Like a crazy person. The pills lift me off the bed. The weight of my limbs stops me from rising to the ceiling. Mrs. du Toit has closed her eyes. Her lips are moving. She's making sounds. I don't know what they mean. I close my eyes too. I don't know how long it is before I want to puke. I force myself off the bed. Stagger naked to my flat. Just make it to the toilet. Drag myself to the fridge for something to get the taste out. There's orange juice. It's off. I retch into the sink. I lean back against the counter. I look at the orange juice bottle. It's not orange juice. It's apricot. It's not off at all. The room is hurtling off its axis. I look at my wall of photographs. I don't have a single picture of Madge up there. I wouldn't know where to put her anyway. The family tree has duplicated itself. One version is at a different focal length to the other. I close one eye. I almost fall over. I make it as far as the couch. My knees give way. I collapse. I wake up. I don't know where I am. I stumble around. I throw up against a wall.

I don't remember Sunday.

MRS. DU TOIT KNOCKS

Mrs. du Toit knocks at my door. She's never knocked with great loud bangs before. I know it's her. The cops would say something like, "Open the door, you're under arrest." It would give me a chance to fling myself out of the window. I haven't seen her since Saturday. It's Thursday evening. I've left work early. I don't feel like going to Eric's. Sonia will be there. She's been bitching at me the whole week. Monday she bitched. Tuesday she bitched. On Wednesday she bitched so much that I snuck out early and got shit-faced at Eric's all on my own. I don't feel like the bitching carrying on under the guise of friendship. Behind the thin armour of beer.

I leave the safety chain on when I open the door. Mrs. du Toit's mascara has run down her cheeks. Her mouth twists. I think of those distraught women from old silent movies. Oversized gestures and grotesque expressions. Her hair is all over the place. She's wearing a grey shape-less thing that's stained wet here and there. She pushes her palms against the door. She wants me to open it. To let her in. The chain holds nicely.

"No," I say. Nobody comes in here. Not under any

circumstances. I sleep with the light on. I eat when I'm hungry. I wash the dishes only when there are no clean ones left. The place is a mess. It's my mess. The mess is logical to me. I have my family stuck to the wall. I can't explain any of it to anyone. I'm not obliged to. It's my last place on Earth.

Mrs. du Toit collapses, almost. She folds more or less in half in the walkway. She clasps her hands between her thighs. She's making a wheezing noise. I think the noise means "please."

"Come," I say. I slip the chain off and squeeze through the gap. Close the door behind me. Take the woman by the arm and guide her towards her door. The door is locked.

"What's going on?" I ask. She turns away from me. She doubles over again and sobs. I can see the wet between her legs as she bends. I wonder if she's wet herself because she couldn't get into her flat. I feel in the pockets of her tracksuit pants. They're also wet. She's pissed on me before. I didn't mind. It's a sterile substance in healthy people. There are no keys in the pockets. There's a pocket thing sewn into the front of her top. I slip a hand in. She's not wearing a bra. I have to wriggle my hand to feel all the way round the pocket. There are no keys there either.

"Wait," I tell her. I go back to my flat. Look for the key she gave me. I hope she doesn't dive over the balustrade before I find it. When I come out she is slumped on the walkway with her back against her door. Her arms are locked around her knees with her head between them. I unlock her door. I pull her up before I open it so she doesn't roll over backwards like a beetle. Just as well because there's broken glass on the floor. Today her flat doesn't smell like coffee and citrus. Today it smells like vinegar and shit. The shards are from a drinking glass. It was empty when it was dropped. Or thrown. There's a plate next to the sink with brown slime on it. Next to it is a mug. It has lipstick on the rim and coffee streaks down the side and some beige liquid in it. In the sink is a pot with spaghetti glued to its sides.

"Is it your tumble dryer?" I ask. Of course it's not. I know that. I just don't know the right question to ask. Mrs. du Toit wheezes again. She's not walking that well. She's struggling to get one foot in front of the other. The arm I'm not holding keeps jerking out sideways. I'm struggling to guide her. I want to slap her to get her right again. I don't. I steer her to her room. There are no flowers on the bedside tables. I seat her on the bed and pull off the grey tracksuit. Top first and then the pants. Some of the wet is sweat. I go to the bathroom to find something to wipe her down. The smell of shit is worse. There's a flannel in the bath and a towel on the rail. I run the tap and wet the flannel. Three pill boxes stand on the vanity. The cards are empty. I feel I should flush the toilet before I call an ambulance. Topping a pile of turd is a thick icing of tablets. They're pink and white and mostly dissolved. Better down the toilet than down her throat. I flush.

In the bedroom I wipe her with the wet flannel. She has stopped wheezing. Has stopped saying "Please." She doesn't resist, even when I spread her legs and wipe with the cloth. There's encroaching growth on the lopsided topiary. I wipe away the mascara smears. I probably should have done her face before wiping between her legs. I do behind her neck and under her arms. Mrs. du Toit has become a compliant laboratory creature. Soft flesh goes this way and that. I wonder how we ever did what we did. How *I* ever did what I did. Without makeup her eyelashes are strangely pale. The roots of her hair give nothing away about its true colour. I lift her legs onto the bed. Cover her. The duvet hasn't been changed for some time. It's soft and slightly sticky. I turn her bedside light on. Open the curtains. There's nothing worse than waking up in the dark. Other than going to sleep in the dark, of course.

"What is it?" I say. I'm scared to ask. I feel I should, though. She's calmer now. I'm relieved when she doesn't answer. I'm about to lock her front door when I realise I have an erection. It could hammer a nail into teak. I go back inside. In the drawer beside her bed I find a vibrator. I place it in her hand and turn it on. It buzzes at about

A-sharp. She doesn't move. Which is the real Mrs. du Toit, I wonder. The one ticking along while her meds are working, or the one crashing and burning without them?

I get up and leave.

In the parking lot I see a couple climbing out of the car. The man is laughing. The woman smiles back. Some things are so normal out there.

In my flat I put my ear to her wall. I strain. There's a faint buzzing sound. It's dropped a semitone or two to A or A-flat since I left. There's no other sound.

"WHAT THE FUCK, Nathan," Sonia says to me on Friday. My feet are on my desk. I'm doodling on Dino's pad. I've taken my phone off the hook.

"What, what the fuck?" I say.

"You're like the living dead, for God's sake. One big sale and it's a holiday suddenly."

"Jesus, Sonia, I'm doing what I can."

"Hardly. I've seen you do what you can. Right now you're doing what you can't."

I put on my sorry face. "Look, I'm struggling here," I say. "It's got nothing to do with the sale." Behind my face I'm wondering how Sonia would look with a Bic pen in her trachea.

She sighs and leans against the cubicle divider. It's not very secure and gives way. She almost loses her balance.

Her little eyes get littler. "It's been, like, two weeks," she says. "It's not like Madge was exactly . . ."

She was going to say "family." I know this. I look at her. I harden my sorry face. Just a bit. I stare at her. I'm challenging her to question my friendship with Madge. She looks down at the floor where my feet should be. If they weren't on my desk.

When she looks up she has her own sorry face on. "If only you knew what I've had to do." She doesn't finish the thought. I can't finish it for her. I wait for her to tell me. She doesn't. I don't know what she's trying to say. I think there might be tears. Her eyes are so small I can't see. She shakes her head and goes to her cubicle.

It's a long and tedious day. I use up all the blank pages of Dino's pad. My doodles get more and more intricate. I'd like to sit here and stipple the view of my cubicle for ever. I toss the pad in the bin. Skip Eric's again. Go home.

I TAKE THE lift. I'm not expecting Mrs. du Toit to ambush me in her colour-coded assault gear. I listen at her door. Silence. I fetch my key and go inside. The spaghetti on the pot has gone hard. The liquid in the mug has grown fur. Mrs. du Toit is in bed. She has cocooned herself in the duvet. She is turned to the wall. Her hair is dank on the pillow. I can smell it. I take her shoulder. "Come," I say, "you need to get up." Why she needs to get up I don't know. Perhaps to eat. To go to the toilet. I pry the duvet from her to make sure she hasn't done so in the bed. She hasn't. She grunts. Grabs the duvet from me and swaddles herself in it once more. I want to look her in the face. I go around to the other side of the bed. She grunts again and pulls the duvet over her head. There is a short length of rope on the floor. It's about as long as a school ruler. Under it is a little pile of newspaper clippings. They're small. Page six stuff. One or two are from the bottom left of a page. Serrated edges where the newsprint was trimmed. Some tell the story of the suicide of Henko du Toit. Some cover his funeral.

It seems Henko du Toit was a financial advisor. He'd embezzled most of his clients' money. When they caught up with him the money had been spent. He hanged himself from an oak tree at his sister-in-law's wine farm. The family was having a braai at the time. They couldn't find him when it was time to eat. Then they did. In the garage. The rope was a guy-line from an old tent. Henko left a wife and a trail of debt and little else.

I replace the clippings. The rope is interesting. I take it to the window and hold it up to the late afternoon light. There's nothing to suggest its history. I sniff it and it smells like rope. Dusty and brown and organic. It must have been a very old tent. I drop it onto the newspaper clippings. I check Mrs. du Toit's toilet. There's nothing to flush. I go to the sink and wash the dishes. Not all of the spaghetti comes off the pot. In the cupboard are three bottles of wine. You'd think her sister would be more generous than that. I take all three to my flat. After the first bottle I compose a resignation letter to Sonia in my head. After the second one I curse Mrs. du Toit. I don't remember anything after the third.

I SMELL PINE needles when I wake up. My pulse is racing. Even when I open my eyes to the sunlight I can feel the darkness of the dream. I lie still until my heartbeat slows. Have a cup of instant coffee. I don't have a coffee machine like Mrs. du Toit. I sit on the arm of the couch and stare at the family on my wall. The pattern of the tree is not symmetrical. I suppose no family tree is. They're all out of kilter in some way. From this angle the woman in the red dress looks like Mrs. du Toit. It's not just the sunglasses. For a moment I feel confused. I look away and my eyes settle on the woman with the big jaw. She still irritates. I take her down. Drop her on my bed as I get dressed. What's worse than her being there is her *not* being there. I stick her into the pocket of my jeans along with Madge's scarf. I'll throw her away later. I go through the photos stacked on top of the TV unit. Find a woman more or less the same age. She has an ugly black thing on her head and she isn't smiling.

I stick her on the wall. I have a great-great-aunt again. She's perfect.

SATURDAY MORNING SUCKS. I watch reruns about aliens. Every now and then I hit the mute button. I listen for sounds from next door. There is nothing. At twelve I heave myself off the couch. Take Mrs. du Toit's keys and go to her flat. The dishes I'd left to dry next to the sink are still there. Mrs. du Toit is also still there. She's still swaddled in her duvet at the edge of the bed. Her forehead is pressed to the wall. The room smells of armpits and hair. There's a half-glass of water next to the bed. At least she's drinking something. I shake her shoulder.

"Come," I say. "You need to eat." She gives the same grunt as before. Except this time she shakes her head. The news clippings and the rope are still on the floor. I shake her again. Repeat what I'd just said. She grunts.

I go to the kitchen and pick at the fossilised spaghetti on the pot. It's hard as glass. I can't dislodge it. I put the pot away with the rest of the dishes. At the end of the counter are her car keys. I haven't driven a car since God knows when. I don't even have a licence.

By the time I find parking near Madge's shop I could probably have walked there or found a tuk-tuk. I'm happy for the car guard to guide me into the bay. Most people hate these guys. I give him ten rand. He thanks me in a

French accent. I have to walk three hundred metres to the shop. I pull my hood over my head. They say the perpetrator always returns to the scene of the crime. Who am I to change human behaviour? It's about fifty degrees. My hair is damp and skanky. I need to wash it sometime soon.

Madge's shop has transformed. There's all sorts of cheap plastic shit in the windows. I go inside. The first thing I miss is the smell. Mildewy dust and tea and wood and leather. Madge's wildly floral perfume. Now, the rubbery odour of artificial fabric smothers me. It's like having your nose deep inside a cheap canvas shoe. A Chinese woman attaches herself to me as I wander down the aisles. As if I'm going to pocket the trinkets and crappy knick knacks on the shelf. I see a T-shirt with a Disney character on it. Over Mickey's head is an arc of cartoony lettering that shouts "Micky Moose." Next to him are "Goofie" and "Donal Dack." I head for the door.

"You not leave, you buy please," the Chinese woman pleads. Or maybe she's commanding. I'm not sure which. It doesn't look like she's smiling. I can't understand her face. I don't have a Chinese face like hers in my library. It's taken barely two weeks to pave over the last of Madge. I don't want to buy, please. I want to leave.

Mrs. du Toit's car knows only two speeds. A low-level creeping and some kind of intergalactic thrust mode. Trying to get it up the hill in one piece gives me a hard-on.

Maybe it's the lurching. Maybe it's the actual driving. I'm trying to get the thing to do what I want it to do. I can't. It's one or the other. Creeping or intergalactic thrust. Somehow I park the beast. I get out and walk around it. There are no scratches or dings. There's at least a metre between the end of the bonnet and the end of the parking bay. I'm sweating. Hard.

I PUT THE CAR KEYS

I put the car keys at the end of the kitchen counter where I found them. Mrs. du Toit is in no state to do anything. There's a lonely unflushed turd in the toilet. At least she's managed to do that much. I find a bowl and some cereal. Strawberry Pops. I thought Strawberry Pops were for kids. I sniff the milk. It triggers an instant dry heave. I go and fetch my milk. It's not much better. I try to feed her. She slurps twice at the spoon. Milk runs from the corner of her mouth. She turns away. Buries her head under the duvet. The duvet is covered in drool stains. I pull it away and try to feed her a little more. She's not interested. I pour the contents of the bowl into the toilet. Floating there it looks like some weird kind of pink vomit. It makes me feel ill. I flush. A dozen or so clump together on the surface of the water. I wait for the cistern to fill. I flush again.

I rinse the spoon and the cereal bowl in the kitchen sink. Leave them out to dry. Lock the door of her flat behind me. Before I've reached my door, I start shaking. Mrs. du Toit has gone somewhere without me. It's not to her sister-in-law's wine farm. It's not to work. It's somewhere in her head where I can't follow. Even when I'm there I'm not there. I may as well be a pot plant or a sheep on a West Coast farm. Or anything else in the world that she's not thinking of. Just like that, she's cut the thing. I'm not sure what the thing is. Whatever it is, she's cut it.

I stare at the TV for hours. I don't know what I'm watching. I wouldn't have noticed if Mrs. du Toit herself appeared on the screen. In a yellow dress or a red dress or a black one. With matching shoes. Yodelling in a talent show. Making a soufflé. Trying to survive in the jungle. People on the TV don't respond to you. They're there at the same time they're not. Some of them are dead. It's like Madge's comment about Steve McQueen. You can watch him shooting and driving on the classic movie channel. Even though he is stone dead. Mrs. du Toit has taken herself to the place where dead actors go. Where you can see them even if they don't see you. She's gone where I can't. Fuck her for going there. Madge too, in fact. Making me kill her like that and then going where I can't.

By five o'clock it's all I can do not to rip my family tree from the wall. I want to start with Woman in Red. I want to tear her into little triangles for her resemblance to Mrs. du Toit. I make myself stop. This family is so new I don't even know them all yet. I need to give them a chance. I feel like setting fire to my head. There's too much going on. There's nothing going on. I can't sit here any longer. On this couch with the bed behind it. With the coffee table all askew between the couch and the TV unit. Its secret drawers, hiding spare members of my secret family. The TV with its endless repeats. The repeats coming back like the things you can't forget.

I take my hoodie from my bed. I put it on while I wait for the lift. My feet lead me towards Eric's. My head isn't interested. I can't do Eric's Alpine drawings and his small talk. I can't do the weekend shift people. The way they do that thing, the journos and the subs. A glance and a half-raised glass and then the ranks that close again. I go to the bar where I went after Madge died. The thought that there will be people there who I don't know cheers me up. The bikers with their posturing and their leathers. Family men in dress-up. Pretending to be who they aren't. Just for an evening. I bet they leave their bikes in secure parking and take taxis home in case of roadblocks.

The worst is when you feel like a drink and it doesn't feel like you. The first sip of my draught is bitter. I can feel the acid of it at the back of my throat. The bubbles are too big. The complimentary peanuts don't help. I wonder whether they'd find traces of urine in the nuts if they tested them. A little bald man tries to elbow his way in to a circle of bikers and their girlfriends. They close ranks and he turns away. He catches my eye before I can look down at my beer. He has a beard that juts like a prize fighter's chin. I stare at the bubbles in my beer so that he doesn't approach. He does.

"Prost!" he bellows, and smacks his bottle against my beer. My glass shatters. It empties its contents onto the counter and into my lap. The barman rolls his eyes. Tosses me a cloth. Cleans the counter with another.

"For fuck's sake, Charlie," the barman says. He throws the cloth onto a shelf behind him. I'm glad my beer has gone. The barman begins pouring me another. I want to stop him. I can't.

"Zaw," the bald man says as the barman turns away. "Zaw zere I vos, in eine grosse unterwasserboot mit eine kleine Volkswagen on de top." The put-on accent is ridiculous. He is rocking on his heels. I want to hit him in the face with his beer bottle. I pull my hoodie over my head. I stare at the empty place where my beer had been. The barman puts a new draught in front of me. He apologises. The glass is not in the middle of the coaster. It's about two centimetres to the left of centre. I push it into the middle. I'm not looking at the bald man. I can feel the weight of him swaying at my shoulder.

"Charlie," the barman says, "give it a break."

I feel a lightness next to me. As if Charlie has been replaced by a fresh breeze. The new beer is cold. It has a crisp white head. It tastes as bad as the first. There's a jug of water on the counter. The ice melted long ago. The lemon has moulted into the water. I ask the barman for a glass. The water has a sour tinge. It tastes better than the beer. I feel a hand flip the hood off my head. I'm ready to embed the glass I'm holding in Charlie's face. The face belongs to a woman.

"I knew it was you," she sings. She's way ahead of me. I have no idea who she is. All I know is that she's at the three-drink stage. At least. I've managed a sip of my first and a sip of my second. She has shiny skin. Her forehead is dotted with pink nodules. She hasn't been a teenager for decades. She's wearing a black leather jacket. The leather is scuffed and greyed at the elbows and shoulders. She pulls up a stool and sits close by. She grabs her hair in two fists and knots it at her neck. She puts a hand on my knee. She leans forward. "I took your fingerprints," she says. "It was me, remember?" I'm not in the mood for this. I try to picture the woman at the police station. A little blue hat pulled low over the brow. An undershot jaw with a Habsburg lip. Slim above the waist. Thick legs made thicker by combat trousers and boots. I look down. Her feet are kicking rhythmically at the air.

"Constable, um," I say.

"Constable whatever," she says. "I shouldn't be talking to you."

"First name?"

"Not even that."

"Can I buy you a drink?" I ask. It wouldn't be smart to

piss her off. She looks at her glass. It contains the last of a dark brown liquid.

I find my smiley face somewhere. "Brandy and Coke?"

She sniffs at the suggestion. "Bacardi," she says. "Bacardi and Coke."

I buy the drink. I shouldn't have. She stays. She talks about her son. He didn't get enough oxygen at birth and isn't quite right in the head. Her upcoming divorce. The arsehole of a husband who didn't know he was on to a good thing. The impossibility of police employees paying their way. The fact she's been a constable for eight years. And will be for the next eight too. The race issue, you see. It's not a career any longer, she says. I need to concentrate to keep up with her. I'm not sure my act is holding up. When the jug of water is finished I wave at the barman for a refill. The head on my draught has gone flat. There are no more bubbles floating through the gold.

There is some kind of aggro-switch floating among the ice cubes in Constable Whatever's fourth Bacardi and Coke. Halfway through, it trips. She removes her hand from my leg. She thrusts her lower lip out. The action pulls at the ends of her mouth and makes it small and mean. She's no detective, she says. Not yet. She doesn't need the rank to be able to tell. I can see her thinking it was *me* that did it. Whatever the CCTV tape shows. She can see it in my face, she says. I'm probably a psychopath. I'm too pretty for my own good. I needed Madge's money for drugs. I dress like a criminal. Who sits in a bar with his hoodie pulled over his head? Who drinks water all night? I'm probably one of those homosexual communists.

I don't look her in the eye. Instead, I put my hand on her thigh. I would really prefer not to. I put on my smiley face again. "Constable," I say. "You're overwrought."

She blinks at the word. I can see she doesn't know what it means. For a moment she's unsure whether to be offended or not. Apparently animals respond to tone of voice. She puts a hand over mine. The lip wobbles. The eyes glass over.

"I'm going to the gents, and then we're going to organise you a ride home."

ON SUNDAY I wake up with the sun in my face. It's March, and still warm in the mornings. Sunrise is an hour or so later than in December. I move my head slowly to one side and then to the other. I expect pain. There isn't any. I remember that I drank water at the bikers' bar. I remember being nice to a policewoman. I don't remember if I finished my beer or not. I suppose I walked home. Either watched TV or went to bed.

I get up. Go for a run. I come home, check on Mrs. du Toit. She has wet the bed. I fight to pull her out of it. A malty smell releases from the sheets. She has nothing on.

I deposit her on the couch and cover her with a towel. She wrestles with the towel until it's bunched under her chin along with her knees. What's between her legs is sexless. Like wood shavings or a handful of parsley. I put the soiled sheets in her washing machine. Before I turn it on I fetch the laundry from my flat. Throw it in with the sheets. I sit on the bathroom floor and watch it spin until it stops. I stuff it into the dryer. I rinse the facecloth and give Mrs. du Toit a bed-bath on the couch. This time I do her face first. I turn over her pissy mattress. On a shelf in a closet I find clean linen. I make her bed. I fetch her from the couch. I collect my laundry from her dryer. I go to my flat. The History channel is starting a new season of *Alien Day*. No repeats. I like aliens. Mostly because there aren't any.

ON MONDAY I STRUGGLE

On Monday I struggle to find my working face. It's March and it's pouring. I wish weather were predictable. We're in Sonia's meeting when the lights go out. The boardroom has no windows. It's like a coalmine at midnight. My heart rate goes ballistic. Sarel flicks a lighter. It doesn't take. He flicks again, and again. The flicking makes snapshots of the faces. I can feel sweat. It pushes through my skin like little drops of molten wax. Sarel's lighter takes. He holds it above his head and uses it to find the door handle. As he reaches for it the lights come on again. It's been a minute or less and still the brightness surprises. Everyone blinks. They clap and say, "Yay." They don't mean it. I'm sure every one of them was hoping that the lights would stay out. That we'd all be sent home.

Sarel sits down opposite Sonia. "Jeez, Nathan," he says. "Scared of the dark much?"

I can see Sonia kick him under the table. What does she know, I wonder. What does she know that I don't? Sarel looks at her and opens his mouth. I suppose he wants to say, "What the fuck, Sonia?" He says nothing. She uses her glare to segue into her usual bollocking. Except she's angrier than normal. We've missed every target ever since the bank thing. The vertical lines at the top of her nose seem to have deepened. When she's finished with us, she starts on the web dev team. They're getting hardly anyone to the site. In spite of the search marketing and SEO work and all the other propeller head stuff the geeks are pretending to do.

After the meeting I'm still shaking. Yumna looks at me as if I'd grown horns or had a haircut. Sarel avoids my eyes. Sonia calls me to her cubicle. I'm going to struggle if she says anything about the lights going out. She doesn't. The nipples declare her mood. She hands me a sheet of paper torn from a pad. The tear went wrong and a long thin triangle is missing at the top edge. On it is a list of names, companies and phone numbers.

"Three things," Sonia says. "One, call these people. Two, remind them that we're still a newspaper that sells half a million copies every day. Three, tell them they'll get 33% off rate card for anything booked and confirmed by the end of the month."

I look at the piece of paper in my hand. The names and numbers are angry. I can't read probably half of them. Sonia hasn't done this since I first joined.

"Want me to give Yumna's and Sarel's lists to them?" I ask.

"They don't have lists," she says. "I want to know how you've done before you go home please."

When Sonia says "please" it doesn't mean please.

I turn to go and walk into Dino. His frame takes up the entire entrance to the cubicle. Just as it fills the cubicle when he's in it.

"'Excuse me?'" Dino prompts as I push past him.

"You're excused," I say over my shoulder.

"Cock," Dino says. Sonia doesn't contradict him. I wonder how much she'd like him if he had one of his mafia crossbow bolts through his temples.

I pick up the phone and start dialling. Dino starts talking. I put the phone down. Blah blah blah, goes Dino. Something about a woman found strangled in the bushes. She must be white otherwise he wouldn't be so excited. Even then it's not such a biggie for him. This is Cape Town after all. All pretty and touristy on the surface, lethal beneath. The locals know that. They know what to stay away from. They know you can lose your life for twenty rand or a cellphone if you're in the wrong place. She must have been a visitor. After almost twenty years, the murder of a white woman still makes the front page. Especially if she's foreign. Black women, coloured women are still page four fodder. Dino's still bitching. The cops aren't giving him anything. Even his closest connections are zipped up tight. They won't let on the who, what, where, when, why or how. "What am I supposed to do?" Dino is saying. "Let the sub write a big headline and then give him one line of copy to go under it?" Grow up, Dino, I want to say. Stop being such an arsehole. Pad it with a paragraph on the weather and some old murder statistics. Interview some people in the area and write that they didn't see anything. It doesn't matter what area it is. It's more likely that they wouldn't have seen anything if it's the wrong area. Nobody will remember the bullshit once you get the real meat in a week's time. I'm listening for Sonia's sympathy noises. She's not making any. She must really have it bad this month. Dino's rant trickles to a stop. I can almost hear Sonia shrug her shoulders. Dino leaves. I pick up the phone again. Call marketing managers and media agencies. Write a blanket email to everyone as I go. Tell Sonia at the end of the day that her list was shit. "It's not the fucking list that's shit," she shouts. She shouts some more as I walk out. Shout shout shout, goes Sonia. I don't know what she's shouting.

I don't feel like Mrs. du Toit. Not today. Not ever again, actually.

ON TUESDAY I plug through Sonia's list again. Every lead basically tells me to fuck off. Either in those exact words or a bit more politely. I wonder if Sonia is setting me up for something. I don't think so. You never know. At the end of the day I've sold some tiny black-and-white ads that will be buried together somewhere behind the editorial pages.

I should tell the clients that they'd be better off keeping the money. That would be the honest thing.

At the end of the day I report my progress to Sonia. "Wow," she says. As if I were a cat bringing her a dead bird. I head for Eric's. Decide at the last minute that I don't feel like it. Don't feel like Eric or the people drinking there. Don't feel like the biker bar. I mooch around town. Pass Madge's old shop. The Chinese woman is standing outside, ordering passersby to go inside. They don't. Then, I don't know what I do.

I wake before dawn. The front of my brain feels like it's been replaced with concrete. It's as if I haven't slept for days. Pine needles, something else in my nose. Some animal smell. For a moment I don't know if my eyes are open or closed. My tongue is stuck to the roof of my mouth. I put my feet on the floor next to my bed. They land in a pile of damp clothing. Running vest. Shorts. Trainers. Moist socks stuffed inside. A pink scarf. Did I get shitfaced somewhere and then go for a mad drunken run? I don't think I drank. I sniff my armpits. They're rank. There's no tang of alcohol. No sour aftertaste of it in my mouth. No fumes of it on my breath. Whatever this is, it can't be a hangover. I should go for a run. I can't think of anything worse. I gather up the kit. It's wetter than it looks. Bundle it with my week's washing under my arm. Find the key to Mrs. du Toit's flat. She won't care if I do a wash. Won't notice in her funk.

I hold my breath as I open her door. I expect the zoo smell I can't get used to. It's gone. The air is still and clean, like a hotel room. There's no odour of shit or sweat or urine. The flat smells like soap and furniture polish. The place is spotless. Even the taps at the sink gleam.

I go to the bedroom. Mrs. du Toit isn't there. The room is immaculate. The bed has been stripped. I open her closet. Clean sheets and the duvet cover lie folded next to her clothes. All crisp and colour coded. I don't see the sneakers and jeans she wore on our walk. I don't know what else she's packed. The rope and the newspaper clippings are gone. I look for them everywhere. In the bedside pedestals and the closet. In the bathroom vanity. In the kitchen cupboards. In every drawer I can find. What I see is perfect order. Mrs. du Toit is hardly a housekeeping Nazi. There is no wine in the kitchen.

I put my laundry into her washing machine. Shower at my place while it's being done. Go back and transfer the load to the dryer. Wait for it to finish. I leave my keys to her flat on a counter. Latch the door so that it locks behind me. Look out at the parking area below. Mrs. du Toit's bay is empty. In my flat I shake out some dryer-warmed clothes. Put them on. Spend twenty precious minutes looking for a tuk-tuk.

I'm late. Sonia says nothing. I can see she's freaking. Her mouth is thin and pulled. She can't look at me. She sticks out a hand.

"List," she demands.

I give it to her. Six of the fifteen items have been ticked off. She looks up at me. "And now?" she says.

"And now I want a new list."

"Why?" she says. "You've been at this one since Monday and nothing. Fifteen prospects, six tiny sales."

"Dog food," I say.

"Huh?"

"You can only sell dog food to people who have dogs. These people have no dogs."

Sonia looks at me blankly. Sometimes she can be really thick.

"Sonia, they don't want to advertise. They don't have the money, or they're doing fine without it, or else they just don't care."

"Remind me what you do with dog food?" she says.

"Sell it?"

She hands the list back to me. "Exactly," she says.

THERE'S SOMETHING WRONG with my desk. There's something wrong with everything on it. I don't want to touch anything. None of it is mine. People like Sarel and Yumna pin things up around their cubicles. Photographs. Silly quotes and cartoons. Kitschy sayings set in Papyrus or Comic Sans. Pictures of random things. Their desks have stuff on them. Their own coffee mugs. Wire bicycles.

Rubik's cubes. Flash drives in the shape of little rubber men or bracelets or credit cards. All sorts of shit. Not mine. There's nothing of mine here. Never has been. I'm sure their drawers are full of rubbish as well. Gimmicky erasers. Bottle openers. Containers filled with useless brown coins. Sachets of McDonald's tomato sauce. More flash drives. I wonder if there's a camera somewhere that's hooked up to my laptop. The thought makes me want to take my clothes off. It's hard enough to sit on the chair. My head is hammering harder than ever. I cross my arms, grab my shoulders. It's like a hug. It makes me feel better. I don't want to let myself go. I sit like that for most of the day. I'm trying to remember Madge and Mrs. du Toit. I'm trying to forget both of them. No, I'm actually working very hard at forgetting them. They deserve to be forgotten. They went away. The harder I work at the forgetting the more I remember them. It's driving me crazy. They're each like a shitty tune you can't get out of your head. Hugging myself stops me from picking up the newspaper's laptop and the newspaper's pens and pencils and hurling them against the wall.

Sonia sticks her head into my cubicle. I don't look at her. At the edge of my vision I can see she has her bag over her shoulder. She puts a hand to her mouth. She drops it.

"Christ, Nathan," she says. She doesn't sound angry any longer. Just tired. "Go home."

I unfold my arms. They hurt from the hugging. I see it's past five. I'm surprised. I wonder what I've been doing the whole time. I don't know. I need to pee.

SONIA CALLS ME IN

Sonia calls me in for a chat on Thursday. I'm late again. I'd been looking for the picture of the woman at the airfield. It's fallen off the wall. You'd think it would have been on the floor. It wasn't.

I expect Sonia to be furious. Nipples at the ready. She's not. Nor are they. She is slumped in her chair. She tells me to sit down. My hands find my shoulders. Sonia looks sad. I don't know what face to put on. I try my smiley face.

"Nathan." She says this and then says nothing for a while. Then she says it again. "Nathan."

I can hear that she doesn't want to see my smiley face. I can hear that she wants me to look at her. I look at her wastepaper basket. It's made of fine black mesh. Somebody must have kicked it at some point. There's a dent in it and the top edge is skew. Inside are a few balls of paper and a clamshell and a can of Coke Zero. The can has leaked brown onto the paper. It's not like the leak is going to attract ants. Ants don't understand Coke Zero.

"Nathan," Sonia finally says. "This isn't working."

You mean I'm not working. I don't say it.

"I don't need to remind you that you were, um, a bit of a special case when we took you on."

Perhaps she does need to remind me. I don't remember. Special implies some kind of incapacitation. Retards are called "special." Maybe that's not what she means.

"You were fine. You did okay. You were almost, almost normal for so long."

I can see where this is going. Or rather, I can see where Sonia is going. She's going away. She's going to go away by making me go away. That's the strategy. I'd bet on it. I turn from the wastepaper basket so that I can't see her at all. I start the process of trying to forget her. There are steps. They're hard enough as it is. They're even harder when the person you're trying to forget won't shut the fuck up.

"I've done everything I can. Now I've lost the fight. At least they've allowed me to give you a choice. One, resign. Two, take a package. Of course, you can fight it if you want to. That'll mean disciplinary hearings, corrective directions, revised performance indicators—and a month or so to come right."

At the bottom of the grey cubicle wall is a big dirty smudge. As if a dog used to sleep against it. I wonder if there are staples in Sonia's stapler. I wonder how much a staple-bindi would hurt.

"You need to know that a fight will just draw out the

process," Sonia is saying. "It's a game you won't be able to win. *They* will, trust me. It'll just be miserable."

Shut up, Sonia. Shut up shut up shut up.

"If you resign," she says, "you won't get any severance. So, as a friend, I'd recommend taking the retrenchment package."

Humans are a stupid design. They can close their eyes just like that. They can't close their ears. Not while they're holding onto their shoulders.

"You'll get two weeks' pay for every year you've worked. Plus they've agreed to pay out your commission on the bank deal until the end of the campaign."

Bye, Sonia. Who would have been allowed to bring a dog to work anyway? Was it an Alsatian? A fat old Lab? An incontinent little Dachshund?

"Nate!" Sonia says. She snaps her fingers. "Sign this." She hands me a pen and a piece of paper. I don't read it. At the bottom is my name and an empty line. I put the paper on my thigh. I sign my name. *Nathan Lucius*. The pen stabs through the paper at the end of the s.

Sonia takes the paper from me. "Okay," she says. She breathes out as she says it. It comes out like a long sigh. She breathes in again. "Let's go to Eric's," she says in her cheery voice. I can hear the brittleness underneath. My hands are holding my shoulders again. I leave her cubicle. Walk past mine. Pass the lift and take the stairs.

I've left nothing behind.

BEFORE

I'M LOOKING AT THE PATTERNS

I'm looking at the patterns in the Persian rug and they're swirling and heaving and making me feel sick.

"Don't you remember me, Nathan?" the woman asks.

I don't have to look at her to see her face. Cheekbones. Little hooked nose. Glasses on and off. Prim dark jacket over a prim white blouse. I know she has her grinning face on. The Persian is spread over a carpet that is a nothing colour. It has deep reds and greens and blues. My eyes zing when I look at the parts where the red butts up against the blue. You could lose yourself in its swirls. Paint yourself the same colours. Disappear into it.

"Come, Nathan. There's lots for us to catch up on."

I keep my nothing face on. There are little sketches on her wall. Thick dark frames with details in gold. The sketches are pencil, pale and grey and barely there. The framer was bolder than the artist. The wall is painted the colour of pot-plant holders. Terracotta, it would have said on the tin. Or maybe Venetian Red.

My name is Nathan Lucius. I live at Number 402, Pansyshell Park, Tamboerskloof, Cape Town. I don't live here. Wherever "here" is. The wind is blowing. It rattles her window. I like to run. I don't have a car. There is a woman who is a widow who lives next door who masturbates all the time. I don't mind. I quite like it actually. She's stopped now anyway. We were friends for a while. For a few weeks I kept her too busy to masturbate. She kept me too busy to masturbate too. Then she went away. Just like that. Cleaned up her flat and left. I don't like it when people just go away like that. Maybe she's back now. Or not. Perhaps she's somewhere else, brewing coffee and drinking wine and drying her clothes. I don't know this other woman behind the desk. The desk is at one end of the Persian. I'm at the other. There is a Persian jungle of colour and swirl between us. When I move the leather of the chair creaks. The dead cow protesting. I wonder if they have cows in Persia. I look at the window. On the other side is only sky. That's why I'm looking at the window. Not through it. Through it is too big. Big blue nothingness that doesn't end. On the glass are splatters of something. It's probably seagull shit. Do you know why seagulls make such a noise when they fly? Because they're scared of heights. The shit helps me look at the window and not at the sky. Then the Persian starts sucking me towards it. I'm being pulled in face-first. This makes it hard to look at seagull shit on the window. In between the big swirls and leaves and lianas of the carpet are tiny other things. Hooky, thorny things. Outside of it all I see the woman look at her watch. Her mouth opens into a slit and air comes out.

"Okay, Nathan," she says. "Same time tomorrow, then."

MY ROOM IS not like my real room. The bed is narrow. I can feel iron through the mattress. The pillow smells like cheese. The window is high and small. There are four bars. No curtains. I'm happy about that. I'm the only one in my room. Most of the others have to share. I am given pills. In the beginning they made me open my mouth afterwards to see if I'd swallowed them. Now they just give them to me. They know I won't spit them out.

Outside of my room everything is grey and yellow. There are bars across doors and steel mesh in the windows. Everything is lit in neon. It's hard to tell if it's day or night. I don't suppose it matters.

THE WOMAN AND I meet again. She reminds me once more that we have lots to talk about. She doesn't say anything to move the conversation along. I could suggest things. Questions she could ask. As in: "Do you know Eric?" Or, "Where do you do your laundry?" I don't say anything. I've decided that I'm never going to speak again. Ever. I disappear into the Persian. I get lost in its swirls and twirls. Then I worry what's behind them. Beasts and snakes and poisonous spiders, perhaps. Scary tropical things like scorpions and jaguars. She sends me back to my room. Again and again.

One day it's different. She stands up and walks through the jungle. The tangles and spirals are nothing to her. She stands in front of me. She has her smiley face on. She stands with her legs apart. Planted in my jungle. She's fearless. The jungle retreats beneath her. I'm impressed. There's suddenly a photograph in her hand. Like she's a magician. It's me at the lake house. Standing in the dappled dark of the pine trees. Like the photograph on the wall of my flat.

"Want to tell me about this?" she asks. She holds it out to me. I don't take it. She puts it on my knee. I stare at the carpet. It helps to chew the inside of your cheeks if you don't want to talk. If you chew hard enough you can taste the blood.

After lunch the two of us walked through the pines to the lake. My sister helped me into the canoe. She told me to sit. She pushed the boat from the shore. It scraped along the brown beach. I could hear the mud squidging in her toes. The mud burped sour gas. I sat as low as I could. All hunched over. She had told me about centres of gravity. I didn't want to capsize the canoe. Isabel laughed before she pushed me off. "Sit normally," she said. "You'll be fine. Just don't stand up." Then she gave the canoe a push. It went straight for a moment. Then it went left. "Sit in the middle," she said. I wriggled to the left. The canoe stopped turning once I was equidistant from each side. Hamish barked. I looked over my shoulder. He ran into the water and stopped when it reached his chest. "Woof, woof," he went in his old broken-voiced way. "Now paddle!" Isabel called.

I dipped the paddle into the water on the right and pulled. The canoe lurched left. I paddled on the other side and it swung to the right. Soon I found a rhythm. The canoe snaked away from the shore. I was the snake-master. Pull left, pull right. "Not too far, okay?" Isabel shouted. I kept paddling. Little waves plinked against the prow of the canoe like bits of liquid metal.

The photograph slides off my knee and lands in the jungle.

It's self-evident, I don't say to the woman. It's me. At the lake house. I'm twelve. There's a dog in the shadows. I wonder if the photograph will get lost in the jungle. If Hamish will be eaten by a jaguar.

"What was the dog's name? Was it your dog?" she asks.

Hamish smells of dust and musk and pine needles and dog. From somewhere there's a smell of chlorine. Or sugar cane. And sweat.

The woman sits down again behind her desk. I stare at

the carpet. She waits. I stare. She opens her mouth a bit. Before the breath comes out I know it's the end of the session. She smiles without her eyes.

"Let's try again tomorrow, shall we?"

SOMETIMES I PLAY chess with Mr. V.J. Naicker. Neither of us cares who wins. The important thing is the playing. The longer the game takes, the better. Mr. Naicker has a black beard flecked with white that they trim back once a month. Like a hedge. He's told me that he's not allowed to trim it himself. He says it itches when it gets too long. I know his history. I know his prehistory too. He paints vivid pictures of the Kerala of his ancestors. He's never been there. Every time we sit down at the board he gives me another chapter. Most of it is coherent. Sometimes he interrupts himself. A comment on the weather. A remark about a politician. A musing on the incompatibility of Hindus and Christians. He says they're like two friendly drunkards giving each other a high-five. They mean well. Their hands miss. He says this often. When he finishes his history lesson he starts again at the beginning. The beginning always loops in just before the end. Just before he is brought to this place. Just as he is about to have dinner with his wife and the daughter he can't marry off.

Sometimes Ricky Chin comes over to watch us at the chess board. Ricky's father was Chinese, he tells us. The apartheid government didn't know what to make of Chinese people. Most of them were here because they wanted to be. Not because they were found here. Or imported like Mr. Naicker's predecessors. They were loaded with business opportunities and tax money. So the Chinese were appointed honorary whites, Ricky says. His chest puffs up. Mr. Naicker snorts and rolls his eyes. "That was the Japanese, and an almighty insult it was too," he says. "They may as well have made you all honorary opera singers. So what's the big deal?"

Ricky puts his hands on our table and leans into Mr. Naicker's face. They're nose to nose. Ricky's arms are hairless. The muscles are stringy and hard under the skin. I see a vein throbbing purple in the crook of his elbow.

"The big deal," says Ricky. He speaks slowly and quietly and his voice rasps. "The big deal is that he was never a coolie like you." Ricky walks off. His legs are stiff. He's like a pissed-off dog. Johnson steps forward. He is one of the nurses. He looks like an American football player or a movie star. His head is shaven. Shiny as a shoe. When he clenches his teeth you can see the muscles in his jaw. Johnson is from Nigeria. He has a great rich Nigerian voice with a great rich Nigerian accent. They say he was some kind of doctor in Lagos. They say he models in his spare time. His medical degree doesn't mean anything over here. I don't know why. Here, he's just a nurse. Ricky

Chin shouts once, loudly. He flails an arm about and he stamps a foot. He bangs on his temples with his fists. Then he flops into a chair. Johnson steps back again. Mr. Naicker's hand is shaking. He puts his bishop into the path of my knight. He has black rings under his eyes. They look blacker than usual. His bishop is unprotected. He shrugs and shakes his head as if to dislodge Ricky's words from his ears. I take his bishop.

THE WINDOWS HAVE

The windows have been cleaned. There's nothing to help me focus on the pane. I look down at the jungle. Her feet are there. Right under my nose. The shoes are shiny and have openings at the front. A toe and a half sticks out of each shoe. The nails are the same colour as her walls. I wonder if she did that on purpose.

"Let's start again, Nathan. Let's pretend we're meeting for the first time, shall we?" From where I'm not looking I see her stick out a hand. Her voice changes. She sounds like Sonia trying to sell ad space to a client. "Hello. I'm Doctor Aphrodite Petrakis. Please call me Aphrodite. It's very nice to meet you."

The hand wavers. It's blurry. I can see it where the jungle disappears at the edge of my eyes. She speaks again in her salesperson voice. "Oh my goodness—haven't we met somewhere before? You look so familiar."

How old does she think I am?

The hand drops. The feet turn and march off. I can hear them as if the rug and the carpet weren't there. The high heels making sharp, angry clicks. At the desk they turn again. Like choreography or a marching manoeuvre. Hup two three—hup. A click click click that isn't there.

She leans back on the desk. She turns and picks up the photograph. She flutters it like a fan. Holds it out to me with both hands. "Do you want to tell me about this yet?" The sales voice is gone. She drops a hand. There's a mug on her desk. She turns again and picks it up and sips from it. If that were my mug it would be full of whisky. I won't tell her anything. She knows it all already. The coyness, the extraction game. It makes me want to grab her by the ears and break her head open against the corner of her desk and distribute its contents across the jungle of her carpet. I try to move. The drugs pin me to the dead cow. It moans.

She puts the photograph down, picks up another. "How about this one?" she says. I look up. I can't help myself. My sister. Her thick hair in a pudding haircut. The bangs an inch deep at least. It's my photograph of Isabel, from my wall. In my flat. Nobody nobody nobody goes into my flat. The possessive is easy enough to understand. Should be even easier if you have a degree. *My* flat. *My* photographs. *My* photographs. *My* flat. Mine mine mine. I look from the photograph to Doctor Petrakis. I will punish her. I will stare at her until something of hers falls out of her. Falls out of her eyes or her face or from under her skirt. I will stare at her until her terracotta toenails drop off. Until her fluids squeeze from her pores. I will stare the breath out of her. I will look at her until something of hers is mine. *Quid pro quo*, you sneaking snooping thieving cunt. You owe me. You take from me, I take back.

Something has docked. Something in the way I'm looking at her, I suppose. Doctor Aphrodite Petrakis teleports herself to the other side of the desk. She reaches under it. I'm not stupid. I know there's a button there. She steps back to stand behind her chair. Like a lion-tamer. The door opens. Johnson comes in. He looks at the woman. He looks at me. He looks at the woman and raises an eyebrow. Her head makes the tiniest jerk in the direction of the door. Johnson comes up to me. He helps me from the chair. He makes gentle Nigerian noises in my ear.

I paddled until my arms hurt. Then I dug the paddle into the water on one side and the boat slowed and turned. I was far away from the shore and from Isabel by now. She was throwing pine cones into the lake. Hamish chased after them and found them in the water and carried them back between his teeth. He dropped them at her feet. Dead ducks. Isabel's new camera hung around her neck. Each time, she held the pine cone to her chest before throwing it. Her elbow stayed close to her body when she threw. I'd shown her a million times how to do it. The camera made it worse. I could always throw further than her, camera or no camera. Isabel, I'd say to her, *you're six years older than me and you throw like a girl. I am a girl,* she'd reply.

I turned the canoe and paddled for the centre of the lake. Soon I stopped and drifted along for a bit. Then I paddled again and drifted again.

Water had splashed into the canoe and my feet were cold and my shorts were wet. The sun burned my shoulders and my neck. Half of me was cold while the other half was hot.

Soon it felt like I'd reached the middle of the lake. I held the paddle in the water and the canoe slowly came around. Then I paddled on one side to turn it completely. Isabel and Hamish were gone. I could see the black roof of the house and some of the white wall beneath. A curtain hung perfectly still out of a dormer window. The dead quietness made all my movements loud. The paddle banged and scraped against the edge of the canoe. The plinking of the water on the hull was sharp and glassy. The air made breathing sounds in my nostrils. I heard Mom laugh from far away. The sound of it rolled through the trees and across the water. When it reached me it was perfectly clear. Just smaller. Mom's laugh squeezed into a little box. The sound made the quietness quieter. Then someone put on Paul Simon. "Diamonds on the Soles of her Shoes." It swallowed the quietness. The sun felt hotter. I wondered if it was Saturday or Sunday.

There is no chess today. Just syringes full of stuff that burns into my muscles. The injections bring on the night. A bright blue moon vibrates through the bars. Shining bright blue in my face. There's a bed under me. There's a sheet over me. It's been turned jellyfish-blue by the moon. The iron under the mattress has been softened by the drugs. Over the grid at the end of the bed there's a gown without a cord. There's no air in here.

IN THE MORNING CHAIRS ARE FLYING

In the morning chairs are flying this way and that. Ricky is being Ricky. He is trying to get out again. Maybe he's not as smart as he makes out. He should understand by now that the bars will always win against the chairs. Ricky is screaming something about needing a woman. There aren't any here. Apparently we all have issues with women. We can't be trusted near them. Old Man Jakes is screaming and wetting himself in the corner. He already has porridge all over his lap. Now it's pee and porridge. The microcephalic Socks Ferreira is hopping from one foot to the next. He claps his hands. He is shouting encouragement to Ricky. Socks shouldn't be here. He's retarded. He's stupid, not crazy. Maybe none of us are. Socks is exciting some of the others. Mr. Naicker sits at a table with his hands over his ears. His eyes are closed. He's told me that commotions make his head hurt. The commotion makes my head hurt too. It hurt before. Now it hurts more. The drugs are okay while they last. It's the wearing off that sucks. I'm slumped on a grey couch that has wooden armrests. The chromed frame supporting the wood is mottled by rust. I wouldn't be able to move if Ricky threw a chair at me. Johnson and the other heavies arrive. One of them is still chewing his breakfast. He has egg at the corner of his mouth. They hang back as Johnson goes in. You can see that they don't want to mess with Ricky. He's a ball of Chinese fire. They've never quite believed that Ricky can't do tae kwon do or judo or something. Johnson isn't scared. He grabs Ricky from behind. Wraps those gymmed-up Nigerian arms around Ricky's shoulders and chest. Slides his arms down, twists Ricky's arms up behind his back. Shoves Ricky forwards until he's on his knees. Then the helpers move in. Take Ricky away.

THERE'S ANOTHER MAN in Doctor Petrakis's office the next time I'm there. "This is Doctor Humboldt," she says. "He'll be sitting in with us from now on."

Humboldt wears a checked shirt and khaki trousers. The checks are made of brown and orange and cream. His gut hangs onto his lap. The cuffs of his trousers have pulled up over his ankles. The socks are grey. The shoes are brown. Soft-soled, slip-on. There's a shadow across his top lip. It looks like a moustache. It's just a shadow. He looks like a farmer. He nods at me. He readies a notepad and pen. The pen is a cheap office Bic. It makes me think of Sonia. It almost disappears in his hand.

"So, Nathan," Doctor Petrakis says. "Have we come along since you and I sat down together a week ago?"

A week. It could have been yesterday. Last month. Last year. I long for the jungle. I see dangerous little things in the swirls. Like thorns. Humboldt's pen hovers above his pad. The windows are dirty again. It must have rained. Dirt spatters the glass in raindrop patterns. The sky is no longer blue. It's grey and low.

"Clearly not," Doctor Petrakis says after a while. She doesn't keep the sarcasm out of her voice. Humboldt flicks her a look. She stands up and comes around from behind the desk. There's a smaller chair next to mine. She turns it to face me and sits down. Close.

"Do you have dreams, Nathan?" she asks. Humboldt writes one word. I bet it says "dreams." Doctor Petrakis is very beautiful. Like a cat. The cheekbones and the slightly slanted green eyes. She has fine parentheses at the corners of her mouth. A little radiance of lines at the corner of each eye. Her hair is so straight it could be Chinese. It has random threads of silver in it. They add an element of gravitas. She sounds like Sonia though. I'm sure she'd be disappointed if I told her that. I'm sure she'd be disappointed if I told her all I want is my flat and my job back. That I don't want to rule the world. It's not what she means by "dreams." She has her soft face on.

"Recurring dreams? Anything that repeats, specifically? By way of images or themes or both?"

I climbed out of the canoe and my bum was wet. I dragged the boat from the water up the shore. The canoe was wide and heavy, and once half of it was out of the water I stopped. A needle of fibreglass was stuck in my finger. It was translucent and yellow and I found it with my teeth and tugged at it. I licked at the little mushroom of blood it left behind. I couldn't get my feet clean. After I rinsed them in the lake I had to go through the mud again. Square One, as Mom always said. This meant going back to the beginning, with no gain. I didn't know what Square One actually, really meant. Why not Square Two, or Cube Three? I thought about this for a minute. Then I realised that if you squared one, you were left with one. One times one is one. You ended up exactly where you began.

I picked up the paddle and my sandals. I walked up to the house and then veered off to the woodshed to put the paddle away. I couldn't get the door open. Isabel had fetched the paddle. She'd bolted the door and I couldn't open it. I leant the paddle against the wall. I went behind the woodshed to pee. Nobody would see me from the house. The shed was made of wooden slats nailed close together. I tried to pee through the gaps between the slats. Pee splashed onto my feet. The world smelled of pine needles and chopped wood. Of dust and grass. And now, a little bit like pee.

Yes, I don't say to Doctor Petrakis. It's a dream of blackness. The blackness smells bittersweet. With mildew in between. Hell isn't made of fire and brimstone. It's made of black. It's chilly and damp. It smells of mould and dust and pine needles. It's made of people.

"What I'm trying to say is this," says Doctor Petrakis. "Do you still have the same dream you told me about when we last met?"

I look away from the dirt on the window. Humboldt has stopped writing. I wonder if he believes her. I wonder if he knows that I don't. I look at her. Look at her hair, her eyebrows. Her mouth. It's pink inside and at the corners where the lipstick has worn off. I look at her chin. At the chain with the glasses dangling from her neck. I look into her lying green eyes. She looks back for a moment and then looks down. She flicks through some papers. She opens her mouth and closes it again. She glances at Humboldt. His huge head makes a tiny nod. She breathes in and then out. She looks back at me.

"What can you tell me about the smell of pine needles?" she says.

JOHNSON HAS TO come for me again. He has September with him. He is almost as big as Johnson. Just fatter. Someone is screaming from far away. The men in the ward stop what they're doing. They're staring at me. And at Johnson and September. Which of them is doing the screaming, I wonder. Next thing I'm in my bed with cuffs around my wrists and ankles. The cuffs are connected to chains. The chains are connected to the iron of my bed. The cuffs are padded. They still hurt. The ward sister comes in. She's new. I don't know her name. She's holding a clipboard to her chest. Doctor Petrakis walks in. Humboldt appears at the door. Doctor Petrakis takes the clipboard from the sister. She puts on her glasses. She frowns at whatever it is that is on the board. She runs the end of her pen down the page. She turns to the sister and her mouth moves. The screaming person is still at it. I wish he would stop. I'm sure there's a medication for that. The sister can't hear Doctor Petrakis speak. Doctor Petrakis taps at the clipboard with her pen. Shakes her head. Points at the page. Holds up two fingers. The nurse nods. She mimics Doctor Petrakis's actions. Doctor Petrakis nods. September and Johnson take my arm and hold it still. The sister has pulled a syringe from somewhere. Doctor Petrakis watches. Then Humboldt squeezes himself against the doorframe to let her out.

MR. NAICKER OPENS with the king's pawn. He moves it two squares towards me. He sips at his coffee. He recoils and blows at it. He waits for me to respond.

"You're not really here today, are you?" Mr. Naicker says. He looks into the coffee in his cup. I'm watching Socks Ferreira. He is sitting the wrong way round on a chair. His hands grip the top of the backrest. He is rocking. Gently banging his chest onto the backs of his hands. Maybe he is staring at the rain streaking the window. I wonder what's going through his head. Not much, I decide. Mr. Naicker is right. I'm deep in a mist of drugs. I'm trying to find something. I don't know what it is. Then I remember. It's the hot coal of anger. I want to hold it again like I did yesterday. Squeeze it tightly in my hands. Feel it burn into my palms. Feel it ignite the rest of me. Feel it burst into a righteous kind of fury. *My* flat, *my* photographs, *my* dreams. The coal glows for a second. It dims again. I repeat: *My* flat, *my* photographs, *my* dreams. The coal glimmers. I repeat the words. Again. Until I'm rocking with their rhythm. Like Socks is rocking with his own list of stuff he's holding onto. The coal has died. It's cold and black in my hand. The drugs are like a fire extinguisher. My flat. My photographs. Flat, photographs, dreams. As combustible as wet socks. Flat, photographs, dreams, anger. All gone.

MR. NAICKER IS suddenly next to me. He's holding two paper cups of coffee. He puts one down in front of me. He puts his hand on my shoulder. "It's okay, Nathan," he says. "I know what they can do to one. I know what they can do to one's head. I especially know what they can do when it comes to the matter of time. They can stretch it or squash it at will. It's a brilliant and magical trick, and it's why people like you and I don't know if it's this week or Christmas." He sips his coffee. "We can give the chess a rest for today," he says. He sits down and packs the pieces away. Then he leans forward. His elbows are on the table and his chin is resting on his hands. "You and I," he says. "You and I need to consider each other as family. Not close family, for sure, because that can be," he says and stops. The empty table helps him think. "That can be, well, counterproductive," he says. "Familiarity and all that. We can be cousins, shall we say. That will allow enough distance for good sense. At the same time, we'd still be close enough to look out for each other."

I don't know what he's talking about.

"It's all about family, isn't it?" Mr. Naicker continues. His hands drop to the table. He looks at Socks Ferreira rocking on his chair. He looks at the rain on the glass behind the bars. He looks at the backs of his hands. "Or it used to be in any event."

I wiped my peed-on feet on the lawn. They still had mud on them. I climbed the steps to the deck. Dad was lying on the wicker couch. Mom and Aunty Mike were leaning with their elbows on the balustrade. Aunty Mike said something and Mom laughed. The laughing made her spill some of her drink into the flower bed below. Hamish looked up at me. He banged his tail on the wood of the deck. I could see that he was too lazy to get up. Isabel came out and took some dishes from the table. She went back into the house then returned for the rest.

"Hey, sailor," Aunty Mike said. He used to have a wife called Aunty Margaret. When I was little I confused the two of them and called him Aunty Mike. That's what they told me. Everyone thought it was so funny that the name stuck. One day Aunty Mike arrived without Aunty Margaret. We didn't see her again. Aunty Mike wasn't our real uncle. We just called him that.

"How were the high seas?" Aunty Mike asked.

"Wet," I said and he laughed.

"I can see," he said. He smacked my bum as I walked past.

"Feet!" Mom said. I went back and rinsed them under a garden tap and stomped them dry on the lawn. Then I went upstairs to change my shorts.

I WONDER HOW RICKY SEES THE WORLD

I wonder how Ricky sees the world through those eyes. It must be like looking through a letterbox. He is sitting in Mr. Naicker's chair. I don't like how Ricky plays chess. He is quick and aggressive. As if the object is to win. To win as quickly as possible. We're on our third game. He's won the first two. I wonder why he's in such a hurry. It's not like he has to catch a bus or hurry to a movie. He twitches so much I can't think.

"Come on, Nathan Lucius," he says. "I haven't got all day." He is sitting on his hands. I wonder if he is trying to control them. His legs are jiggling up and down. If you strummed him he would play D-sharp. I don't know where he thinks he's going.

"Where's old man Naicker today?" he asks. He looks up at me. I think he rolls his eyes. It's hard to tell. "Stupid," he says. "Asking you." Then he stops jiggling. "Just take that pawn already, okay," he growls. He doesn't wait. He reaches out and takes his pawn with one of mine. "You don't mind, I'm sure," he says. Then he jumps his knight into no-man's land. "Go," he says. "Go go go." I didn't want to take his pawn. I have no idea why he's placed his knight where he has. He would have time to think if he didn't rush. He starts jiggling again. Then he stops and leans forward.

"Do you know the story about Naicker?" he asks. He is whispering. It's louder than if he just spoke normally. Then he says, "Fuck it," and his hand darts out and moves my bishop two squares to threaten his knight. "Naicker gets home from work one day. He greets his daughter and kisses his wife. The wife is making dinner. I would have fucked her for first course if I had a wife. Fucked her for mains too. Anyhoo, he goes to the bedroom and takes off his jacket and his tie and his shoes. He puts on his slippers and goes down for dinner. I definitely would have fucked his daughter. Fucked her for starters, mains, dessert and the cheese platter." Ricky puts his knight into retreat. He leaves it up against the left margin of the board. "His wife has made a leg of lamb. She asks him to carve it. He goes to the sideboard. He starts carving and his daughter tells him about her day at the consulting firm. She's yakking on about her work when old man Naicker turns around and slits her throat with the carving knife. His wife jumps up and starts screaming, so he stabs her five times in the chest and once in the eye. Maybe in the eye first and then in the chest. Nobody knows. Then, he carries on carving the lamb. The neighbours hear the wife scream and they call the cops. When they get there . . ." Ricky stops and moves my second bishop. His knight is under threat again. "When they get there, the cops I mean, old man Naicker is sitting calmly at the table eating roast lamb with a side of mash and peas. He's even poured himself some juice. And added ice. His wife and daughter are in their chairs, stone dead and bleeding all over the place, and he's just sitting there, chowing away."

Ricky glares at me. I wonder if he's waiting for me to challenge his story. He moves a pawn randomly on the right-hand side of the board. He grins. "That's us," he says, "a hundred and fifty percent cuckoo crazy, every one." He suddenly remembers his exposed knight. He looks down to confirm his mistake. "Fuck!" he says and slaps himself on the forehead. He takes his knight with my bishop.

I'M WAITING

I'm waiting for Doctor Petrakis. She's late. Humboldt is in the room. He is writing on his notepad. I don't think he wants to look at me. He could be writing a shopping list. Milk, bread, grey socks. The windows have been cleaned. There's new rain on them. Humboldt's tan shoes are mottled with wet. As if he's walked through grass in the rain. I'd like to do that very much. To walk through the grass in the rain. Except I probably wouldn't wear shoes. I'd even run barefoot on tarmac for an hour right now. I think about Ricky and Mr. Naicker and Madge. If Ricky thinks he knows all about Mr. Naicker, what do Ricky and Mr. Naicker and Socks Ferreira and the rest think they know about me? It's a village in here. Every story has a nub of truth. Smoke and fire. I can't remember all the other clichés. Still, Ricky's story about Mr. Naicker could be complete bullshit. The truth is probably half as bad. There's probably bullshit that's being shared about me as well. About Madge. Because I'm here because of Madge. I *know* I'm here because of Madge. Somehow, somewhere, someone found out. The careful CCTV selfies notwithstanding. The difference is that I'm not certifiable like

Naicker or Ricky or Socks. I did Madge a favour. She asked me to. She asked me to because she was sick and in pain and not dying. I wish Doctor Petrakis would cut to the chase. Open the door on Madge. Maybe I'd even talk to her then. I'm sure I would. If she promised to leave alone everything else that is mine. Everything that belongs to me.

I'm thinking these things when Doctor Petrakis walks in. I've never seen her in a rush before. She's bent slightly forward at the hips. Her bum sticks out. She has a sheet of A4 paper in her hand. "Sorry," she says. "I was waiting for this." She's a little breathless. She can't be very fit. She goes to the front of her desk and leans against it. She holds up the paper. The picture on it has been printed by a printer with calibration problems. Sonia has bands of white across her face. Her nose doesn't join properly in the middle. I look at the rain on the window. It falls in little fits. There's a sudden spattering. Then there's silence. Then another wave of wet.

"Your old boss tells me she was concerned about your memory. I was wondering if this was just her perception, or if you've been aware of any memory problems?"

Her question strikes me as sneaky. If I do have memory problems, how would I remember having memory problems? And how could I possibly vouch for the validity of Sonia's opinions? Sometimes the drugs do this to me.

Instead of the mist, they bring about a sharpness. Not that it matters. I'm not going to say anything. Not to anyone, ever again. It's surprising that Doctor Petrakis hasn't understood this yet. All those certificates on her wall. She needs some sharpening drugs herself, I think.

I yawn and snuggle deeper into the chair. The leather has warmed up. I put a leg over the armrest. It's comfortable. I could stay like this for ever. It's probably more comfortable than Doctor Petrakis would like. Outside it's grey and wet. I bet Humboldt's feet are cold in their wet socks. He probably hates winter. Me, I would have gone for a run in the rain. Come home and had a hot shower. Wrapped myself up in warm things. Pansyshell Park wasn't made for the cold. I'd have watched movies for hours. Had a wank. Fiddled with the family on the wall. Made sure their faces, their personalities, logically lead to mine. Tweaking the genetics. For now, I'm happy enough to be in Doctor Petrakis's room. It's dry. It's warm. I still can't figure out the pencil sketches on her wall. One looks like a bird. Or a ballerina with her leg extended. Too bad the frame is squashing on her from all four sides. A bit of music would be nice. I wouldn't know what kind I want. Something sleepy. Piano, maybe. Now and then, like now for instance, I would like to open my mouth and speak. Purely to point out the obvious. How could I remember, if I have memory problems? Asking me if I remember memory problems doesn't make sense. However sneakily it's phrased. The actual truth is, I can't remember. Can't once remember Sonia bawling me out for my memory. All sorts of other things, definitely. Never memory. I can't remember, so how would I know?

It's a boring session. Doctor Petrakis skirts around things. I get half of what she's skirting around. The rain stops. Humboldt yawns with his mouth closed. It stretches the bags under his eyes down his cheeks. It's not pretty. It makes me yawn. Doctor Petrakis too. I wait for Doctor Petrakis to start a question with the words, "So how did it make you feel?" At least she spares me that.

MR. NAICKER IS back.

"I've been a little under the weather," he says as he sets up the chessboard. "So it's nice to see you again." He scratches under his jaw. His beard has been cropped short. This should make him look younger. It doesn't. The skin under his eyes is darker than before. I'm sure the lids are thicker than they were. While the rest of him has somehow grown thinner. He lines up his pieces. His hands shake. He knocks over his king. Johnson comes up and removes his paper cup of coffee. Mr. Naicker rights his king. Johnson comes back with a cup of water.

"Thank you, Johnson." Mr. Naicker looks at the paper

cup and sighs. "Such are our pleasures reduced, here by the rivers of Babylon."

We begin to play. We take our time. Each of us willing the other to win. Or at least not to lose too quickly. Ricky Chin must be under the weather today. He's not around. Socks is watching *The Simpsons*. He guffaws. I try to connect his laughter to what's happening on the screen. I can't. There is none. I suppose he's laughing at *The Simpsons* because he knows that other people do. I wonder what he did to be here. What Ricky did. What the rest of them did—Old Man Jakes, Mr. Naicker, Simphiwe with his dark skin and yellow eyes. Me. I watch Mr. Naicker's hands. They're age-appropriate. He's touched my hands before when he's chosen a fist. The skin of his fingers is as soft as a girl's.

"You never talk," Mr. Naicker says to me. "In fact, in all our time together in this wonderful place, you haven't said a word. I'm not questioning the value of your company, no, not one bit. And I'm not saying you aren't polite. A nod is as good as a wink to a fallen soul like me. I suppose you know my entire long history, the official parts anyway, and yet I know nothing of yours."

Qe5. Check. I rap on the table and point to the board to alert Mr. Naicker to the danger his king is facing.

"Did I mention that I was Christian? A descendant of the long-ago converted Keralite heathens. Catholic, actually, with all the guilt that comes with it. Maybe you would feel easier if you knew I was a Christian?"

Mr. Naicker looks at the board for a long moment. Then he moves his bishop. It takes him out of check and places me in it. "Funny," he says. "We've been Christians for generations. In spite of that, I don't think I'd ever eaten beef before I got here. Lamb, mutton, venison on occasion. Anything except beef. Beef, I have to say, tastes like paper when overcooked." He peers at me. "Did you know your face never changes?" he says. "You have a phenomenally straight face. 'Poker' doesn't even begin to describe it. I win, I lose. You eat, you don't eat. One day you watch a comedy on that crappy TV, a tragedy the next. The Stormers win, the Stormers lose. Ricky goes bananas. Ricky offends people. Ricky disappears for a few days. Socks soils himself. Whatever. They fill you with drugs. They double your dose. They take you off the drugs. V.J. Naicker talks, questions, does his best to entertain and amuse. Also disappears for a few days. Whatever. You don't ask, you don't comment, and your face doesn't change. You're like someone who's had two strokes, one in each hemisphere of the brain."

I look at Mr. Naicker. I decide to reward him. I look right into those great wet black eyes of his. I put my smiley face on. Over my smiley face I put my laughing face. I've learnt that the two work best together. Mr. Naicker's eyes grow wide. Then I laugh. It's a laugh I haven't used since I laughed with Sonia and her friends at Eric's. Whenever that was. It was generally noisy at Eric's whenever I was there with Sonia. My laugh had to be a loud one. Else why bother? From the blurry corner of my eye I see Johnson starting to twitch. I run out of breath and my laugh winds down.

"Jumping Jesus, Nathan," Mr. Naicker says. His voice sounds like his throat has dried up. "Stop it. That's just plain goddamned scary."

I let my face go back to normal. Normal is probably a nothing face. The kind of face you have while you make coffee. Or just before you brush your teeth. Normal is nothing. I sit back. I see Johnson relax and lean back against the wall. Mr. Naicker looks down at the board. His forearms are resting on the edge of the table. His hands are shaking worse than before. He looks up at me. He is close to tears. "Please, please, please don't ever do that again," he whispers.

When I came down Dad was asleep on the couch. Snores came out of him like they did from Hamish. Loud and not in time. The table had been cleared. Aunty Mike still had his elbows on the balustrade. Mom had turned around and was leaning against it with her bum. She had kicked her shoes off. Their glasses were full. I sat on the top step next to

Hamish. Mom and Aunty Mike were talking. It was boring listening to them. Every so often Mom laughed her rolling smoky Mom laugh. Dad didn't even flinch. I could see his underpants up the leg of his shorts. I rubbed Hamish's ears the way he liked. Then I stood up and called him. I could see he didn't want to play. Slowly he scrambled up. We went down the steps and across the lawn and into the pines. It was hot even in the shade. Nothing grew under the trees. There was just an endless carpet of pine needles with old cones and sticks jutting out. I threw a cone for Hamish. He yawned and lay down and rolled onto his back. I scratched his tummy and his chest and under his chops. His tail swept pine needles from one side to the other. One of his legs kicked. Riding the bicycle. I picked up a stick. I got on my knees and scraped away at the pine needles. Perhaps there was treasure here, I told myself. Pirate treasure from the Lake Pirates. The earth smelt damp and insecty under the detergent smell of pine. Underneath the needles the ground was hard. The stick broke. There's no treasure here, I thought. No such thing as Lake Pirates. I threw the stick away. Hamish stood up and shook the pine needles from his back.

JOHNSON TELLS ME

"Johnson tells me you had a good laugh the other day," Doctor Petrakis says. "Didn't it feel good to laugh again?"

It felt like laughing. It didn't feel like anything else.

"I wonder what was so funny?"

I'm wondering my own shit. I'm wondering if they've changed my meds. I feel like talking. Specifically about Madge. There's a problem. I'm ninety-nine percent certain I'm here because of Madge. What if I'm here for something else? Like that thing of hugging myself. That thing I did during my last few days at work. Maybe it was weeks, even. Maybe somebody didn't like that. And then there's the not talking since I've been here. The hugging thing was nothing. Just a bit of holding myself together. Like the not talking thing. The not talking thing is a strategy. I'll tell them all the things I want to tell them once I know what it is they want me to tell them. Killing Madge was definitely a thing. I can't be the one to start talking about her. I need Doctor Petrakis to ask me about her first. Otherwise I'll be admitting that I killed her. I'm not stupid. The meds haven't fucked me up completely. I know that killing her because she asked me to doesn't make it legal. No matter how much pain she was in. I wonder whether Doctor Petrakis is as clever as the glasses on her face and the certificates on her wall make her seem. She makes me wonder this even more deeply by asking another wrong question.

"Did you laugh often before you came here?"

Goodness, as Madge would have said. Now it's about *laughing*. Or not laughing. Or some kind of measurement of laughter. Maybe you measure laughter like you measure ad space. The number of men who walk into a bar across, multiplied by clown noses down. It's clear outside today. Doctor Petrakis's scarf tells me it's cold too. If she had half a brain she'd wear a pink scarf. A pink scarf would be a signal to tell me that it's okay to talk about Madge. A deep pink scarf of silk would be exactly right. Doctor Petrakis's scarf is black and sheer. It looks acrylic. It's probably cashmere. I don't have Madge's scarf any more. I suppose somebody else has it now.

Doctor Petrakis stands up behind her desk and walks towards Doctor Humboldt. I hadn't noticed him until now. He's become part of the furniture with his beige pants and dull shirts. Doctor Petrakis is wearing black stockings. They whisper to each other as she walks. Whsh whsh whsh, they go. She bends over and cups her face to Humboldt's ear. Secret things. All this beating about the bush. I look at the Persian for points of interest. There's nothing new there. I have to work hard to see the jungle in the patterns. I've never had to work at this. It's hard to get the picture right. It just looks like a carpet. Maybe it's because I'm wondering how long I've been here. Whether it's been weeks or months or longer. I don't know. I wonder whether Mrs. du Toit is still doing herself in her flat at Pansyshell Park. And doing it more often. In my absence. The thought should make me horny. It doesn't. Nothing does these days. It's probably the meds. It would be nice if Mrs. du Toit visited. Perhaps she's found someone else to do her. I think about Sonia. One two three kinds of bollockings to the crew and nothing really changing. It would be nice if Sonia visited. Madge couldn't visit even if she wanted to. Seems that once people go away, they stay away.

Doctor Petrakis is standing over me. "Do you want to talk about Adele du Toit?" she says. It's the closest she's come to perspicacity in all our time together. I don't answer and force myself to think of Madge some more. Madge Madge Madge, I scream in my head. It doesn't work. Doctor Petrakis's telepathic moment has passed. She goes back to her desk and writes down a few words. Then she purses her lips and breathes out hard. It's the end of the session.

I walked back to the house. I didn't really want to. There was nothing to do under the pines. Least of all find Lake Pirate treasure. And Hamish so old and lazy.

I was at the edge of the trees when I saw Aunty Mike and

Mom. Mom had her bum against the balustrade. Her dress had hiked up. I could see the white skin of her thigh. Aunty Mike had an arm around her back. Mom's arms were hooked around his neck. They were kissing like people in a movie. I hated movies where people kissed like that. Tongues and spit and someone else's teeth. I always closed my eyes when those scenes came on. It was worse than watching people being shot. People being shot was okay because mostly they deserved it. And the blood and the bullets were fake. Everyone knew that. You couldn't fake a kiss, though. Not even in a movie. I'd never seen Mom and Dad kiss that way. Definitely not on the deck after lunch.

I shouted for Hamish as loudly as I could. I knew he was standing next to me. He looked up at me with his head on one side and an ear up. I shouted for him again. Huh? said his face. I shouted and shouted and shouted and then I stopped. Mom had turned around. Now her front leant against the balustrade and she was looking out over the lawn. Her arms were crossed. Aunty Mike was almost next to her. He looked at the pines as though he'd never seen them before. Just like Mom. Aunty Mike picked up a glass. He tossed a few bits of ice onto the lawn. When he saw me he took a sip from his empty glass. I tried to play the fool with Hamish as we crossed the lawn so that I wouldn't have to look at them. Hamish was too old for tackling and tumbling and things. He wasn't interested. He trotted back to the house and I had to follow him. His tail was wagging. Like he was happy at the thought of lying on the deck and doing nothing.

When I got to the steps Aunty Mike straightened up. He took Mom's glass from where it was balancing on the balustrade. It was also empty. Aunty Mike went to the drinks trolley. He picked up a bottle and held it out and peered at it and waggled it and peered again.

"Shit," he said.

Dad's eyes flicked open and closed again.

"What, Mike?" Mom said.

"We're out of gin. And it was turning into such a G and T afternoon."

Mom looked at Dad. She put a hand to her forehead and shook her head. She went to the door and stuck her head inside. "Isabel?" she called. "Isabel!"

Isabel's hair was all tangly when she came out. She yawned and scratched at her hairline and rubbed her nose with her wrist and frowned at Mom.

"Come," said Mom. She held out the keys. "I'm a bit squiffy, so you'll be driving."

Mr. Naicker has disappeared again. If they cut his beard any shorter they may as well just shave it off.

"Shock therapy," Ricky says. "Ouch."

Ricky and I are playing chess. Or rather, I'm watching him annihilate my pieces and his.

"They take these electrical things and attach them to your head," he says. "And then, ka-blam, it's like Frankenstein. A gazillion volts into your brain."

He takes my bishop with his knight and his knight with my queen. NxBe7. QxNe7.

"Ka-*blam*," Ricky says again. Shouts it. Makes a slow-motion explosion with his hands on the *blam*. It's as if he can actually see shrapnel flying from his fingers. He watches the invisible debris as it settles to the ground.

Johnson starts circling. Ricky calms down.

"It's like flushing your brain. Clears out all the shit, just like that. So for a while you're fine, until it clogs up again. And then, ka-*blam,* all over. What do you say to that?"

I want to say that it's not 1969. What next, lobotomies? I say nothing. I never do. The chessboard is in a pickle. I can see that Ricky is stumped. Maybe he's forgotten which colour to move. Or which part of him wants to win, or not lose, which is black and which is white. He shoves the board aside. Kings and queens and bishops go head-over-heels. Some pawns survive. Then he smacks the board with the back of his hand. The rest of the pawns fall. Ricky does that Ricky thing and stands up and plants his hands on the table and leans over it.

If I had the energy I would take one of the fallen kings and drive it into his eye.

Ricky hangs his teeth out at me. "Silence isn't a defence,

Nathan Bloody Fucking Lucius," he says. "You can shut the fuck up all you want. It doesn't mean it didn't happen." He throws himself back on his chair. Puts his hands behind his head. Lurches forwards again. I struggle to focus on him.

"So how did it feel, little man?" he asks.

It feels like I want him to shut the fuck up. I look at the board. I want to play chess. I want to play chess with Mr. Naicker. The pieces are all over the place. Scattered and senseless. Lying sideways. Chess only makes sense if you stay in the squares. It's not that I want to win. I just want a long, slow game of chess. I miss Mr. Naicker. I miss his civility and his calm chatter. It gives you a sense of being. Like a radio that you're not really listening to. That's not going to go ballistic and start screaming, or stop suddenly, unless you turn it up. Or off. I miss Mr. Naicker's understanding that the longer the game is, the better off we both are. Neither of us is the aggressor. The winner is the one who makes the least mistakes. If I make the mistakes, he wins. He lapses, I win. If we don't take all day, we start again. We line up rows of pawns and rampant horses and horny bishops and impotent kings and go at each other again. Slowly, patiently, as if we'd just invented the game. As if we were testing it out for the first time. Bloodless bloodshed. The gentlest of wars. The truth is, neither of us is very good. We only know so many opening moves between us. We've tried to invent new ones, with instant and disastrous consequences. Which means the game is over long before it needs to be. When that happens you have to start again. It's tedious. Like washing your clothes only to get them dirty again. It gets you nowhere. So we forego the innovations. Stick with the traditional openings. Play the way we know. No surprises.

"Come, Nathan," Ricky Chin says again. "Really now—how did it feel?"

I'm still looking at the board. I'm willing the pieces to take their places. It's not working. There's a quick shadow. Something goes crack. It's Ricky. He has clapped his hands, loudly, in front of my face.

"You see now," he says. "I clap, you shit yourself. You are not deaf. So you're not dumb. You just don't want to speak."

I look for Johnson. He's leaning against a wall with his great gymmed-up arms crossed. He's got a foot up on the wall behind him. He's listening to September with his head to one side. Johnson laughs. Simphiwe is asleep in a chair. Old Man Jakes is staring at the empty trees outside. Johnson Johnson Johnson, I scream in my head. He's as useless as Doctor Petrakis. I reach out and swipe the chessboard off the table. It clatters to the floor. The pieces spill across the linoleum. Ricky Chin closes his eyes and shakes his head. Johnson stops laughing. He unfolds his arms. He comes over to us.

"Sorry, Johnson," Ricky says. "A little accident. Caused by this little prick."

Johnson puts the board on the table. He scoops pieces off the floor with his huge black hands. Ricky rebuilds the board. The black king is broken. He's now the size of a pawn. The top half of him can't stand up. Imagine having to defend two kings. Ricky puts the king's head on the table. "Nice one," he says. Johnson goes back to chat to September. Ricky has decided that he is white. He moves his king's pawn two squares towards me. My dwarf-king seems hardly worth defending. I push his pawn out a square. Defensive stuff. Ricky ignores the move.

"So, Mr. Lucius," he says. I'm waiting for him to move. He doesn't. "So," he says again. "How did it feel? The scarf around the neck, the tightening, the ending of things?"

I don't want to listen to Ricky. I look at Johnson. He's talking to September again. I don't like Johnson any more.

"Two for you, almost three. Let's call it two and a half," Ricky says. He laughs and leans forward again. "I fucked you up on that score, Nathan Lucius. Seven for me. *Seven.*" He leans into my face again. "That's what they think. Just seven. Arseholes. No fucking idea." I have no idea either. No idea what he's on about. He leans back and puts his hands behind his head. "Seven to your two and a half. Poor fucking show, Lucius. A little bit like your chess." Ricky jumps a knight over his row of pawns. I place a finger on the stump of my broken black king. Push it over onto the board. Ricky doesn't like that one bit.

"No!" he screams. "You you you you *you!*" he smashes his fists onto the table. The chessboard flies up. Lands. "*You!*" Ricky screams again. "You do not capitulate!" He leaps up. "You do not just fucking give up!" His chair falls over backwards. He turns and screams and kicks it. The chair skitters across the floor. Socks is standing in the middle of the room. He's swaying gently and gaping at something. Or nothing. The chair hits him on the shin. Socks starts screaming. He grabs his leg and starts hopping up and down. Then he lies on his back clutching his shin. He screams even bigger screams. Old Man Jakes opens his eyes and looks around. He starts bleating like a sheep. Apparently he's not that old. He just looks that way. War will do that to you. It will make you old and bleat like a sheep. Ricky leaps up. He flaps his arms and bellows and stamps his feet. Then he goes for the chairs again. Johnson and friends unpeel themselves from the wall.

I WANT TO KNOW

I want to know where Mr. Naicker is. It's raining and Humboldt's Hush Puppies are stained dark again. They squeak when he walks. I imagine variegated toenails in soggy socks. The toenails hooked and digging into neighbouring toes. I shake my head to make it go away. I look for Sonia in the jungle. One thing, two things, three things. When Hamish died we got Suzie. She was a Doberman. She was nothing like Hamish even though she was a dog. She hated pine cones and swimming. She didn't like her tummy being scratched. She never banged her tail on the deck. Her tail was only as long as your thumb, anyway. Suzie's name was wrong for her in so many ways. I put my nose to hers one day and she snapped and growled. We weren't friends after that. Perhaps docking her tail was the problem. They've redone my meds again. It's like being drunk and sober at the same time. Drunk happens within parameters. You know when you are and when you aren't. You know where you are when you're drunk. You know what works and what doesn't. With the meds some things work fine and others are complete toast. As soon as I try to make a point in my head it's gone. The point and the argument leading to it. I think my point was about people. Poor forked animals that look more or less the same. When they're all so very different from each other. I know that's not profound. That something there was borrowed from Plato. I can't remember what I was trying to say. It was something about not seeing people. As individuals I mean. You tend to see at them as one thing. A single great biomass. You have to make a real effort to see them as individuals. It's hard to look into someone's eyes and to see the backstory. The things that worry them. Like indigestion and dandruff and stools that aren't quite right. Diabetes and money and poisonous spiders. Flickering pinpricks of dreams that were once flaming beacons. Deaths past and deaths to come.

Doctor Petrakis starts asking the wrong questions again. She got it so nearly right with Mrs. du Toit when it should have been Madge. Today I'm hoping for Sonia or Mr. Naicker. It hardly matters anyway. I can hardly keep my eyes open.

Blah blah blah, goes Doctor Petrakis. I'm really not on the planet. I know she's not actually saying blah blah blah. I can't wedge myself into her words to the point where I can understand them. All I can tell is that there was a question in there somewhere. She may as well be asking me about the atomic values of the periodic table or interrogating me on cuneiform. Whenever my eyelids droop the jungle dims.

I've just remembered my point.

My point is that everyone is different. I know that's not a particularly insightful point. What I'm trying to say is that Suzie was a dog and so was Hamish. Suzie was different to Hamish in every possible way. Even though they were both dogs. I'm not saying that Sonia and Mrs. du Toit and Madge and Doctor Petrakis are dogs. Or bitches. I'm not some kind of primitive misogynist. Some kind of lower-order Neanderthal. I'm talking symbolically here. You expect a modicum of constancy among people. It's not unrealistic. You expect dogs to be basically consistent. To demonstrate similar behaviours. You expect them to be loyal. To eat their Hill's. To love their walks. To shit on the lawn. You'd be really thrown if your dog started demanding apple pie with crème anglais and began crapping in the guest toilet. Or if it painted your house green of a morning. So it's logical to expect the people in your life to share some kind of common behaviour. Display some kind of follow-through. Some shared traits. Even if they are different people. Sometimes I expect too much, I suppose.

My other point is that they'll always think people are crazy if they keep filling them up with drugs.

THE CARPET PUSHES out an octopus of tendrils. I try to count them. I can't. It doesn't matter. They're warm and soft and free of thorny bits. They poke their spongy ends into my ears. I'm in my bed in Pansyshell Park. The sun is beating down on me through the window. In stereo I hear the glassy plinking of little waves against the bed as it drifts out into the lake. The bed isn't a bed any more. It's Doctor Petrakis in moulded fibreglass. I'm sitting in the hollow of her back. I'm paddling as quickly as I can. Her face is in the water most of the time. I'm scared that if she drowns so will I.

MR. NAICKER IS back again. They haven't shaved off his beard. What they have done is make him younger. The black bags under his eyes have disappeared. His face has lifted. As if the skin has been pulled back and tied in a knot at the back of his head. I check. It hasn't.

"Nathan, my boy," Mr. Naicker says as he sets up the chessboard. He sounds like a motivational speaker. All lightness and spark. Someone has taped the black king up with Sellotape. Stickiness has leaked onto the body. It makes the king stick to my fingers. Then the stickiness is on my fingers too. "There's nothing like a court case and a good bowel movement to clear the mind," Mr. Naicker says. He folds his hands over what remains of his paunch. Then he unfolds them. He spreads his arms wide as he embraces the common room. "This," he says, "is my new kingdom. It will be mine for the rest of my days. And you, Nathan, are my prince. Even though you've been sleeping solidly for almost twenty-four hours. Even though the learned might get the dosage wrong from time to time."

I don't know what he is talking about. I move a pawn a square ahead of my queen. He pats my hand. "It's all good, Nathan. All good." I don't feel like chess today. The slowness of it. I feel like a run. A run along the mountain road with its marshmallow breeze. It's raining again. I can see streaks on the window panes. Winter in the Cape. Horizontal sluices that let up for a moment and then pelt again. It seems the world is underwater. I'd take it. I'd take a run in the rain right now. I'd take the blisters that come from running in wet shoes. The running vest pasted to my chest by the wet. The chafed nipples and the shrunken dick. The icy air setting fire to my lungs. I don't feel like playing chess in this grey-yellow room with a crazy man who killed his wife and daughter. They didn't ask for it. Right now I wouldn't mind running barefoot around the broken lawns of this place with a chain tying me to Johnson. I'm thinking how to tell this to someone. I'm thinking this when Johnson comes up to our table. I hope he's going to invite me for a run.

"You have a visitor, Nathan," Johnson says.

I blink at him.

Mr. Naicker bangs on the table with the flat of his hand. The chess pieces dance like they're on coals. "We're playing a game at this particular actual moment, Mr. Johnson," he growls.

"And you can carry on afterwards," Johnson says. "It's not like you're going anywhere soon."

It's a bad week for the chess set. Mr. Naicker flips the board into the air. The white queen hits me on the forehead. The other pieces scatter. Some land on the table. Most fall to the floor. Mr. Naicker scoots his chair back and puts his forearms on the table. He clenches his hands as if in prayer. I can't tell if it's Hindu or Christian. He puts his head on his forearms and begins to weep. Not so much of a motivational speaker, then. September comes over. Johnson walks me towards the visitors' room.

It can't be Madge. Madge has gone. It's probably not Mrs. du Toit. I'm hoping it isn't. We were all about fucking, Mrs. du Toit and I, not talking. When we talked neither of us listened. We would just wait for the other to come up for air if we wanted to say something. Anyway, I couldn't face Ricky Chin's leers. Or comments about her colour-coding. It might be Sonia, though. Sonia coming to bitch that I haven't made my targets. To invite me to Eric's. Either way, at least I'd have an excuse.

The visitors' room is through a grey door. The paint is shiny. Set into the door is a little window. There's wire mesh sandwiched in the glass. Through it I see the top of a woman's head. The brown hair is streaked with honey.

I don't know who it belongs to. I don't even know if she's sitting or not. It's just a window with some hair in it. I've never been into the room before.

Johnson unlocks the door and pushes it open. The woman looks up. She's grown so old. The smoker's lines around her lips disappear when she smiles. Her lipstick has leaked into the crevices. Up towards her nostrils. Down towards her chin. The eyebrows push up wrinkles. She never had wrinkles on her forehead. Or the tributaries around her eyes. The deep brown of her eyes has watered to khaki. Her eyes are rheumy. There might be glaucoma. The sight of her makes me smell the pine smell of gin the pine smell of pines. It makes me smell the lakeshore fart and the grease of old dog. I want to do terrible things to her. Bleeding, stabbing, kicking, painful, terrible things. I don't know which of the things to start with. I try them all at once. Johnson brings his great sculptural arms and grabs me around the shoulders. I try to elbow him. It's kind of laughable. If you weren't me. If you were just watching from somewhere. If you were watching a skinny runner being wrestled to the floor by a giant Nigerian. Johnson hooks his arms under my armpits and yanks me up. I kick at his shins with my heels. Kick kick kick. I hear someone screaming. The screamer is off down a long tunnel. It could be a man or a woman. It could be Ricky Chin or the woman in the room or Johnson himself. I can't tell.

I kick backwards to bury a heel in Johnson's balls. He's too tall. I whip my head back to smash at his face. I want to rupture his lips against his perfect teeth. I want to break his nose. Shatter a cheekbone. Crack a skull. Black an eye, at least. I try twice. Twice I miss. Johnson locks my arms behind my back. It feels like my shoulder blades are pressing on my cranium. He's pushing my head forwards. The full Nelson. Next thing I'm kneeling on the floor. I struggle. My knees slip on the linoleum. My face presses against its alien rubber skin. Johnson has knotted me like a pretzel. I'm useless. "Come on, Nathan," Johnson says, "how far, my guy?" Which is Nigerian for "what's up, my man?" Johnson's words are gentle. Deep and thick. He isn't angry. If I had to think about it, I would hate how Johnson never gets angry. I'm not really thinking anything right now. I have my arms trussed behind me. I have my face smeared into the lino. Anger is not going to work here. I make myself relax. The more I relax the more he will. And the moment he does I'll whip round and gouge his eyes out. I'll tear his fucking tongue from his mouth with my teeth. I'll rip his polished skin from his skull with my fingernails. Johnson has done this before. I know he feels me relax. So he doesn't. More nurses run up. They take my feet, my arms. One holds my head by the ears so that I can't turn and bite at fingers, arms, faces.

Hamish lay down on the deck. I sat next to him and rubbed his ears. Isabel drove Mom off in the BMW. I could see that Isabel wasn't pleased. She generally drove like she threw pine cones. Like a girl. Now, grit flew up behind the car and the dust rose and drifted into the highest reaches of the pines. Dad threw a forearm over his eyes. The pitch of his snore dropped. The dust hung in the stillness between the branches.

Aunty Mike watched the car disappear. He took a sip from his empty glass. He looked baffled and put the glass down. Then he turned to me. "Nathan, my boy," he said. "It's time you and me have a man-to-man talk." He wasn't grinning and laughing and joking. I didn't want to talk about him and Mom. I was trying to forget. I was telling myself that I hadn't in fact seen whatever I'd seen from the forest. While Dad snored. If Aunty Mike talked about it I would just look at the floor and nod.

"Come," said Aunty Mike. "We're going to have a little chat." He held out a hand. I didn't take it. I stood up on my own. He put the hand on my shoulder. He steered me down the steps and onto the lawn. We could have talked right there. On the deck. Mom and Isabel had gone off to town. It would have taken more than Lake Pirates or a volcano to wake Dad up. Aunty Mike nudged me across the lawn towards the shed. He took the paddle from where I'd left it against the wall. Maybe he wanted to teach me about paddling. He'd need an

actual paddle for that. All he said was, "May as well put this away while we're at it." He tugged at the bolt on the door. As usual, it stuck. He yanked at it and it slid aside. He pushed the door open. The cool smell of pine logs and mould washed out into the heat. "Step inside, Nathan," he said. He pushed me into the solid dark of the shed. "This is just the place for us men to discuss the ways of the world."

"Your mom was a little disappointed yesterday," Doctor Petrakis says. She puts on her glasses and looks at some papers on her desk. She takes up a pen and makes a note. At the same time Humboldt writes on his pad. I wonder if he's making the same note. Doctor Petrakis takes her glasses off. She puts them on again and takes them off. My chair creaks. The thing with the glasses is driving me nuts. Either she needs them or she doesn't. The onning and offing tells me she's not sure either. I feel like a good long run. A run into the wind. In the rain or under the sun. I want to run to Egypt. I'll stop only for water and a crap. In between I'll just run. I'll eat when it's safe to do so. My head hurts. A run to Cairo would clear the drugs from my veins. Clear my head. I'm atrophying from all the chess. From all the sitting. If I can't run I'll swim. To Perth or Rio. The further I go, the warmer the water will become. Or else I'll fly. Flap my arms all the way to Delhi or Budapest or to Boise, Idaho. Anything to clear the wool from my brain.

I don't think I'll be running or swimming or flying any time soon.

I follow a spiral in the carpet as it curls in on itself. Then I follow it outwards. In again. Out again. My eyes are scanners. Scanning this way and that. Hunting for predators. I am a robot in a Tom Cruise movie. Being a robot makes my head hurt less.

Doctor Petrakis puts on her glasses and takes them off. She clasps her hands under her chin. The glasses hang from her fingers. "Were *you* a little disappointed, Nathan?" she asks across the jungle.

Finally she's asked a right question.

I open my mouth and move my tongue. It's like a sock. A thick runner's sock freshly out of Mrs. du Toit's tumble dryer. Fluffy. Designed to suck up moisture. I open my mouth wider and a little croak comes out. I clear it away. Swallow the stickiness. I try again. It's not really my voice. It's high-pitched and weird. It doesn't matter. It works.

"Not as disappointed as I was when Aunty Mike fucked me in the woodshed," I tell her.

DOCTOR PETRAKIS DROPS

Doctor Petrakis drops her glasses. They slip from her hands to the desk. The rest of her doesn't move. She's pretty good. Just not that good. It was Ricky who got me talking. Not her. Ricky talks a lot of shit. Sometimes it's hard to isolate the good bits. What he said yesterday was pretty smart. About silence not being a defence. He had a point. So I'll talk. I'll tell them things. I'm not telling them everything. They'll have to ask more of the right questions first. Humboldt has a snuffly way of breathing. I realise that because it's suddenly silent in his corner. I don't know what he's doing there anyway. He's not only badly dressed. He's superfluous.

"So you remember, then?" says Doctor Petrakis, picking up her glasses. She can be glad I'm full of drugs. I'm instantly furious. She's known about the woodshed all along. All the while playing a stupid game, when she knew all along. What a cunt, I think. I imagine two stiff fingers thrust into the softness where her collarbones come together. I'm not going to give her the pleasure. Not now. Not yet. I shrug. Ricky was the one who got me talking. *She's* the one who got me to remember. Photographs and pine needles. I've spent twenty years trying to forget. I've spent every minute since then teaching myself not to remember. Twenty years' worth of time. Of stuff. Of beer. Whisky. Work. Wanking. Anything to bury that day. Doctor Petrakis's question is redundant anyway. Perhaps rhetorical. Plain stupid, even. Or just some words to give her time to rearrange her brain. All this time to get to what she already knew. Jesus. She might have asked a real question. She might have asked exactly what I'd been trying to bury. Then she'd have had me.

"It's time to get up," Mom said to me after my third day in bed. I was lying on my stomach. She threw the sheets off me and pulled my bumcheeks apart. It still hurt to go the toilet even though the bleeding had stopped. I didn't care. It didn't matter if my arse hurt or not. It didn't matter if it rained or the sun shone. If I was missing school. If a great big asteroid was a mere hour away. It didn't matter that Mom said Aunty Mike would never visit again. He was there all the time. Especially in the dark. There was only one way to get rid of him. Open the curtains and put a light on. This wasn't an either/or. It was both together. That's why it was one thing, not two. Getting up was the last thing I wanted to do. I wanted to lie there for ever. With the curtains open. In my room in our city house. Where the air smelled of cars and fishy harbour and wet tar when it rained. Not of pine needles

or dust or lake fart when you walked through the mud. Mom rolled me over and took me by my forearms and pulled at me until I was sitting up. She took my uniform from the closet and tossed it onto the bed.

Mom and Dad must have been talking for a change. She said exactly what he'd said to me the day before. "Come, Nathan," she said. "School. It's time to put your brave face on."

The pink tip of a tongue creeps out from between Doctor Petrakis's lips. It plays there for a moment. As if she is tasting what she wants to say before she says it. Perhaps because she is going to come straight to the point for a change.

"Nathan, let's go back to our very first meeting. We established that no counselling had been sought for you in the years following the lake house incident. Do you remember that?"

I shrug. It's part of my new vocabulary, I decide. It's cheaper than words. I decide that it will mean whatever the other person wants it to mean. Like, "If you say so." Or, "I don't care." Right now it means "I don't know." It's a convenient addition to my library of faces.

"Do you remember those early sessions? After your troubles at varsity, I mean?"

I shrug again. This time the shrug means two things. Both "I don't know" and "If you say so."

"And can I assume that since we last saw each other, you haven't discussed the incident at the lake house with anyone else?" Doctor Petrakis is losing it again. She should ask me a question that requires a proper answer. Not a "yes" or a "no" or an "I don't know." She should offer me some water. My tongue still feels like a sock. A sock wrapped in another sock, deep in an underwear drawer. She's making notes. She's scowling through her glasses. Or over them. Which is where the scowl happens. Scowling over them and looking through them at the same time. I'm sure the pen is tearing the paper with every underline. With every stab of a full stop. I can see that she's angry. Then she looks up. She smiles. If she's angry, she's not angry with me. For a change her eyes smile with the rest of her face. I'm almost disappointed.

"Well done, Nathan," she says. "See you tomorrow."

THERE'S ONLY ONE picture hanging in the common room. It's held into its frame by a sheet of plastic. No glass in here among the lunatics. I've never looked at it. It's hung too high up, the way some people hang artwork in their houses. Way above your line of sight, like laundry above an old European street. Maybe that's why I've never bothered to look at it. I take one of the grey chairs and push it towards the wall. Johnson tenses. I suppose he thinks I'm going to do a Ricky Chin. Throw the chair around. Or at him. I push it up against the wall. Its rubber feet have long disappeared. The chair grates along the floor. Socks moans and flaps at one of his ears. There's a new guy in today. He's fifty or so. Big, with orange hair. He's spent most of the day staring at his hands. They're freckled. The fingers are short and broad. Sausagey, like a farmer's. He pulls his neck in at the sound of Socks's moaning. There's already not much of a neck. Now there's less. I stand on the chair. Johnson relaxes. In the frame is an old photograph. I see the grain before I can decode the black-and-white image. Me and old photographs. We know what we're talking about.

The photo reminds me of my family on the wall at Pansyshell Park. Not because there are people in it. There aren't. Just because it's an old photograph. Of an old building. It could be a Herbert Baker. Or a disciple's. Adapted colonial, someone once called the style. I don't remember who it was. Great thick walls. A sense of symmetry. Grounded and belonging. Windows that always look smaller from a distance than when you're close up or inside. The building in the photograph is big. Not Groote Schuur big. Big anyway. There's a tower that rises above the building. Like a great squared stake that's nailed the place to the ground. The tower has arches at the top. Like a belfry. The arches recede into darkness. There's a pitched roof over them.

Either it was dark on the day or the photograph is badly

printed. In the foreground are trees that all bend in the same direction. The photograph is cropped. You can't see the ends of the building. The crop makes it look like the place goes on for ever. The whole thing is such a cliché. A madhouse out of a horror movie. At least I know where I am now. I squint at the dark arches of the belfry. I'm looking for bats. I stop looking before I don't find them. It would be a pity if there weren't bats.

I climb off the chair. I grind it across the floor to the window. Johnson tenses again. It's boring. I'm not going to do anything. Mr. Naicker is sitting alone at the chessboard. I can feel his eyes on me as I pass by. I can feel the longing in them. Socks moans and drops to the floor, cross-legged. He puts his hands over his ears and starts to rock.

At the window I stand on the chair. It's not easy to see through the mesh. The window isn't the cleanest either. Still, I can make out a highway at the bottom of the hill. I watch the cars for a while. For no good reason I pick out a black Range Rover and follow it. Even through the grime I can make out a blonde woman in the passenger seat. She's probably beautiful. Women in Range Rovers usually are. And thin. I'm sure that her handsome and successful husband is driving. There's probably a child in the back. Maybe more than one. They're probably all singing along to a CD. Off for a holiday or a weekend together. Even when I think hard I can't decide what day it is. Between me and the highway are trees. They're not very tall. They all grow at the same weird forty-five degree angle to the ground. The southeaster will do that. I wonder which of the windows in the photograph I'm looking out of.

Then Ricky is tugging at my trousers. They're not really trousers. They're pyjamas that have an elasticated waist. With each tug he's exposing an arsecheek. Ricky is excited. Then, Ricky is always excited.

"Come on, come on," he rasps. As if we have a plane to catch. I'm tired of people telling me to come on. I get off the chair. Scrape it away from the window. Ricky pulls me to the chess table by my arm. Pushes me into a chair. Mr. Naicker has disappeared. He has left the board set up for a game. "I'm white!" Ricky says and does nothing. For a moment I think he's talking about the honorary Chinese thing. Then he opens with a pawn. Instead of two squares he moves three. "Did you see the new guy?" he says. He looks at me a moment. "I can't believe I'm asking you questions. Like you're going to give me an answer. Anyhow, you couldn't miss him. Big. Fat. Ginger. Burned down a building with his sister in it. Shot his old man in the head. Then burned down the family house. With the old man in it. A low score, sorry for you, Ginger. What a way to do things. Took them months to find the old guy."

Ricky grabs one of his knights and jumps it over the row of pawns. He takes a pawn from my side of the board.

Bangs it over two squares as he counts, "One! Two!" Releases his queen by pushing the king's pawn two squares up. Forgets to play for me. Sends his queen streaking out of the blocks. "Who's on top?" he yells. "Me. Me me me. Seven up. Leading on goals and on aggregate. Followed by Nathan No-speak at two and a half. Fuck Ginger. I'm the poster boy here. Substance trumps style every time. Seven trumps two, trumps your pathetic two-and-a-half every time. Fucks you up at chess as well."

Ricky isn't making any sense. I move my queen out. Then my bishop. I don't need to look at Ricky to know that his mouth is hanging open. I grab two handfuls of his pawns and thrust them towards myself. Only one stays standing.

"Nathan, for fuck's sake, you're ruining the game," Ricky whines. I'll show you fucking ruining, you twisted little cunt. I take my back row of heavies and push them all forward. I take a bishop off the board. Mine, Ricky's, who knows? I make a fist. I stick the bishop's mitre out between the knuckles of my first and second fingers. I punch Ricky in the chops. The bishop buries its mitre in the flesh of his cheekbone. For a moment it hangs there. Then it drops to the floor. Ricky's cheek has a hole in it. Then the hole wells up with blood. Ricky is frozen in space. He is staring at me. The blood overflows the hole. It runs down his cheek. Ricky puts his hands to his face and howls. He pushes back on his chair. The legs stick on the linoleum and he goes over backwards.

"Checkmate," I say. Nobody hears. Ricky's screaming too much. Everything is good for a moment. I have my anger back.

OF COURSE THEY UP MY MEDS

Of course they up my meds again. I suppose I make it hard for them. Sweetness and light one moment, standing up for myself the next. Mr. Naicker tells me this. I agree with him. We're sitting on the grey plastic couch. He doesn't feel like chess right now.

"I felt the weight of a thousand worlds lift from my shoulders," he says, "the moment I'd cleansed myself of my family. Society sees this cleansing differently. Society seeks to revisit my original burden and to turn it into a burden of a different shape and description. Have you ever done judo, Nathan?"

I shrug. It means no. Mr. Naicker's eyebrows fly up.

"Ah. After all this time, a communication. Which I shall take as yes, no or maybe. And regard as progress nonetheless," Mr. Naicker says. "Anyway. In judo, as I understand it, you are taught to use the weight and force of your opponent to your advantage. If he comes flying at you—and forgive my primitive way of putting this, having never done judo myself—you are trained to manipulate his strength and speed against him. Presumably by stepping aside and tripping him. Or using his momentum to fling him into the wall behind you."

You can use judo when you play chess too, I want to tell him. Just ask Ricky Chin.

"My point being," Mr. Naicker is saying, "that when they come at you with their own version of history, which they will, rather like a bull in a bullring, you should simply step aside as a matador would. Flash your cape at the bull so that it merely spears air. Use the energy of its charge to drive your picas deep into its back. Judo-style." He consults the ceiling for a moment. "I do believe I am mixing my metaphors," he says. "Nevertheless, I'm sure you understand. My actual point being," he continues, "that we are here to get better. While we have each of us transgressed in some way, this is not the place for further misdemeanour. The place for that was in our previous lives. The things we did before arriving here must *stay* out there. As if we'd been in Vegas. If you transgress in Vegas and you are caught, you will serve your punishment in Vegas." He smiles and lifts an arm as if in benediction. "So in here, our challenge is to be calm. To let the drugs do their work while we meditate, contemplate and heal. To take comfort in what we achieved before they put us here. To enjoy the peace those achievements bring. Let the disturbed and distraught shout, for we are safe in the knowledge that their tantrums are not directed at us. Let the doctors throw medications and psychobabble at us, and let us make it work towards our individual wellbeing with our clever judo tricks."

Mr. Naicker looks at me. I've been staring at the feet of the red-haired man. I'm wondering if he could walk across burning coals and come out unscathed. I'm wondering just how mad Mr. Naicker actually is. As in, where would he sit on the Ricky scale of one to completely batshit. Mr. Naicker pats my forearm. He smiles. I can't help myself. I like Mr. Naicker.

"Here endeth the lesson," he says.

You're expected to go to university. So I did. Dad was paying. If I'd had to draw a picture of him it would have been of a guy in a suit with a credit card as his head. He went away when I was, like, twelve. One day he was there and then he wasn't. Left Mom to entertain a string of Aunty Mike clones. At least they stayed away from me. I gave the first ones a hard time. It took time for me to understand that none of them wanted to roger me in the woodshed. Not that we had a woodshed any more. Or a lake house. Those went when Dad went. Nobody was sad. Not about the house or the man we called Dad. Dad, the stuffed Polo shirt. Soft-cock Dad. Then Isabel went away too. She found a dentist. He was everything a dentist should be. Short, efficient, depressive. Procreative. Isabel sent me an email when I was at varsity. Dad's dead, the email said. And it said a bit more about booze and rehab and a liver that more or less imploded. Good, I wrote back. Good to know that I'll never again have to take it up the arse while he's asleep. While he's passed out on the couch and his best friend is tearing my rectum apart with his giant dick. And Dad doing less than nothing afterwards. Other than giving advice. Put on your brave face, sister dear. Bye, I wrote. I never heard from her again.

The next day I came out of a Tech lecture with a headful of numbers and dreams. Bridges with minimal environmental impact and affordable housing schemes for the poor and airports that actually worked. The usual undergrad stuff. Excited, and exciting. Nobody had raised the dead ends yet. Nobody had said that reality was doing alterations to Mrs. Jones's bathroom. Or debating conservatory layouts with Mr. Smith, or spending three months trying to get plans through the City Council.

Next was Architectural History. Stuff we should have known anyway. I was doing a non-credit course in furniture design and the lectures clashed. I knew my Michelangelo from my Wren. So I went to the furniture design lecture instead. The lecturer was late. She always was. She'd keep us waiting at least fifteen minutes before arriving in a great brown caftan that was meant to hide her bulk. If hell is a place of our own devising, mine will be a place of waiting. Don't make me wait. I'd rather climb Mount Fuji on my knees than wait. Or my elbows, even. My forehead, in fact.

I made a point of never sitting next to the same person in lectures. I was there to graduate, not make friends. The guy who sat next to me that day looked like a B Com student. Rugby-ish. Totally wrong for Arch, pronounced Arc. Then there was the furniture design module. Us arty-intellectual types with our little rectangular glasses and polo-necked sweaters. Way superior to the rest, we Arch students. There was the need for food and water. And then there was us. Shelter. Beautifying your shelter was the first step to sublimation. That first handprint on the cave wall. Dogs and antelope could find food and water. Only we could build a roof. Fuck me if we weren't brilliant. Or on the way to brilliance.

Rugby Boy looked me up and down. He lifted the corner of a lip. He was smirking or laughing or something. I didn't know what.

"So," he said, all quiet and secretive, "should I bend you over the desk and fuck you right here, or should we skip this shit and head for the gents?"

I suppose some rugger-bugger B Com types are bona fide gay. That's fine by me. I don't mind gay people. I don't judge them. It's illogical. When, say, Student X comes into class, you don't snigger behind your hand and say, ooh, she likes it doggy style, and then deny her any career or social prospects because of that. You don't deny rights or privileges because of some minor paraphilia. Ability and talent are seldom connected to the way people deploy their genitalia.

Some of the rugger types spent their lives looking for a fight. They'd seek out gays and then beat them up. I didn't *know if this one was trying to pick me up or insult me. Or genuinely wanted to fuck me. It didn't matter either way. You didn't decide without my input that I should take it up the arse. Not more than once in my lifetime anyway. It's why I was expelled from res in my first year. There was a head-butt and a broken nose. He was an Arts student, which is probably why I wasn't expelled outright. I looked at Rugby Boy. He was barely twenty-two and already the drink was showing on his complexion. Tiny blossoms of veins flowering on his nose. Yellowed eyes. I found my smiling face. He grinned back and I felt for my digs key in my pocket. It was newly cut and sharp as a saw-blade. I embedded it in his neck. Attending the lecture was a med student considering a switch of degree. Lucky for Rugby Boy.*

So that's why I was thrown out of university in my third year. I kind of understood. I was sent to Doctor Petrakis. I told her, among many other things, that the guy was like Aunty Mike. She pretended to see the similarity. There wasn't one. Not at all. He was just some boozy denialist coward trying to get laid by an Arch student while his rugby buddies weren't watching.

There is a flip chart on a stand where Humboldt used to sit. At least the chart commands attention. Some of the pages have been flipped back. I wonder what's on them. Whatever is worth writing down is generally worth hiding.

Doctor Petrakis is almost cheerful. "So, Nathan," she says. "How are we doing today?"

I shrug. I'm liking this shrug. I like that it can mean anything.

"Good, then," she says. "I hear, by the way, that you've had a bit of a fallout with Ricky Chin?" I shrug again. Yes, no, maybe. She's working hard at ignoring the flipchart. All it does is make the thing more interesting.

She comes from behind her desk and leans her butt against the front of it. She crosses her ankles. There is an insufficiency of calf muscles. A little bandy, too.

"Mike Bauer," she says. "You called him Aunty Mike." My tongue is a sock again, stuffed into a trainer. I can't move. Can't shrug. "He was arrested five years ago and put away for grooming and paedophilia. Twenty-five years, so he has another twenty to go. That means you'll be over fifty when he gets out. If he lives that long. He'll be well over eighty by then."

I don't need her to do the maths. All I know is it's not enough. Whether he dies there or not. Not enough for what was swept under the carpet. The jungled thorn-infested beast-ridden carpet. Can you get rid of a carpet like that? With all that stuff under it? Surely some dark residue will always cling to it. Will always bring its contamination with it. Wherever it goes.

I manage a shrug.

"Okay," says Doctor Petrakis. She goes over to the flip-chart. I'd never before noticed how broad her hips are. She flips a sheet over. Underneath it are two images. Madge on the left, looking young and healthy. On the right Sonia, badly printed. Doctor Petrakis takes a blue marker from the tray. She draws a slow blue circle around Madge.

"Do you know why you're here?" she says.

I ASK DOCTOR PETRAKIS

I ask Doctor Petrakis for a glass of water. It's the third thing
I've said in God knows how long. She buzzes for a nurse
and September comes in. He nods and comes back with a
paper cup filled with water. I can see it won't be enough. I
drain it before September is out the door.

"More," I say. "Please." September looks around at me.
His eyes are enormous. The whites are not as clear as they
should be. He turns to Doctor Petrakis. She tells him to
bring a jug. He looks at me again on his way out.

Doctor Petrakis draws another blue circle around
Madge. "We were saying," she says. "Do you know why
you're here?"

It's difficult to talk, even after the water. My mouth feels
like somebody else's.

"She asked me to," I say.

Doctor Petrakis drops the marker. I know straight away
that I've given the wrong answer. Even though it was correct. I should have said, "Because Madge's death made me
sad." And let her take it from there. Doctor Petrakis goes
down on her haunches to pick up the marker. She keeps
her knees together and pointed away from me. Ladylike.

She wobbles a little once she's up. As if she stood up too quickly.

"I see," she says. She goes to her desk. September comes back with the jug. Doctor Petrakis pours herself a glass of water. She has a real glass, not a paper cup. She sits at her desk and drinks. Then she looks at me and raises her eyebrows.

I tell her about Madge. I can't stop. I don't leave anything out. She's taking notes. There's no stabbing and tearing at the paper now. Just speed. I wonder if she knows shorthand like Dino. I decide she does. Any notion of stealing her notepad is completely pointless. When I get to the evening of granting Madge's wish I break off. My tongue is sticking to my palate. I stand up and go over to the desk. Doctor Petrakis reaches under it. "No need for that," I say. "I'm not going to do anything to you." I pour myself some water. I think she blushes. I drink all the water in the cup and fill it up again. I go back to my chair.

I've just finished the part about the funeral when she looks at her watch.

"It's time, Nathan," she says. Her voice has gone soft and so has her face. "We can carry on next time."

"Can I ask you something before I go?" I say.

"Of course."

"You didn't know about me and Madge?" I can see she

doesn't want to answer. She doesn't want to look at me either. "You said I could ask," I remind her.

She breathes in and out. She looks at me. "No," she says. "I didn't." She crosses her arms.

I feel a smile on my face. I shake my head. "Stupid," I say.

"I beg your pardon?"

"I'm not talking about you," I say.

"A LITTLE BIRD tells me you've begun to speak," Mr. Naicker says. A big brown bird, more like. I wish September had kept his fucking mouth shut. I shrug. We're sitting at the window watching the rain. Mr. Naicker has crossed an ankle over a knee. The anklebone has thick black veins in relief. They burrow away from the bone and up towards his calf. It's cold in here. I wonder why Mr. Naicker isn't wearing pyjamas under his gown.

"Ah. So the words are only for *in there*." he says. "No matter, then. Perhaps there will come a time when you'll deign to speak to me too." He sounds peeved. I don't care. I'm not really listening to him anyway. I'm trying to think. I'm trying to imagine why Doctor Petrakis would have a picture of Sonia on the same flipchart page as Madge.

I'M BECOMING IRRITATED

I'm becoming irritated at having to wait for Doctor Petrakis all the time. I have things to say. Her tardiness makes the fifty-minute hour even shorter. She is late again today. When she arrives she is holding a mug of tea. It's a kind of chai or herbal something. It steams. The steam releases the fragrance of citrus. Doctor Petrakis's eyes are watery. I wonder if she's been crying. I can't imagine it. She takes a wad of tissues from her bag. She peels off two and blows her nose. I think I remember reading something about the Japanese never blowing their noses in public. They think it's disgusting. I agree. Even if what I read wasn't true. Or I remembered wrong. Blowing your nose should be done behind closed doors. You wouldn't take your dick out and relieve yourself under the dinner table. Why is it okay to expel snot? Doctor Petrakis finishes blowing. She balls up the tissue. Then she dabs at her nose with the ball. Drops the ball in her bin.

"Apologies, Nathan. Midwinter sniffles," she says. She sniffs as if to prove it. Midwinter means late June. That means I've been here three months. How time flies when you're full of drugs. June makes sense. It's raining again. Straight down.

Doctor Petrakis sips at her tea. She takes the mug over to the flipchart. My pictures aren't there. She flips through a whole lot of sheets. Most have writing on them. I try to read some of it. Some sheets have diagrams. She's flipping too quickly. I can't decipher anything. The scribbles must be about other patients. I'm not sure I like that. I realise I've had this notion about her. That she only exists when I'm around. Springs into life purely for our sessions together. Like some kind of automaton. I don't very much like that she has a life outside of this. It's unpleasant to think about it, actually. I've always known that she's married. The ring could be some kind of shrewd automaton disguise, though. I suppose it makes sense that she leaves the building at the end of the day. Gets into her car and drives home. To one of those big old Rondebosch houses. Not too far from here. Just far enough to forget about her daytime job. I'm guessing that she lives there with her husband. Let's say he's in asset management. They discuss household budgets and the leaves that clogged the swimming pool all through autumn. By now the leaves will be gone. The trees will be bare. The water in the pool probably tending to green. Perhaps she has children. I look at her standing at the flipchart. I try to imagine children emerging from those wide hips. From the confluence of those slightly bandy legs. It's disgusting. Perhaps those same children have trouble with homework. Or get tonsillitis from time to time. When she's with them she's probably not thinking about me. She puts them to bed and then she fucks her husband. She might even have a lover on the side. "Working late, darling, the lunatics are trying today." It can't be Humboldt. Nobody could be with Humboldt. Except maybe a dugong. She might have hobbies. She looks like she reads. She might play golf. Or be a watercolour painter. She knows so much about me. I know nothing about her. The only thing I now know is that she doesn't switch off and die at the end of our sessions.

Doctor Petrakis flips over a page and there they are. Madge and Sonia. She looks at the pictures. She's thinking. Her cold has probably slowed her brain down a bit.

The first time I was here it was different. There was no Ricky or Mr. Naicker or Johnson or September. I don't remember Humboldt being around. Who would? Only Old Man Jakes was here. And Doctor Petrakis. She was younger then. Obviously. Not as broad across the hips. Didn't need glasses. I think she is more beautiful now than she was back then. She had a different room. It was smaller. Painted the standard institutional beige. The oak desk was scuffed and scarred. Like an old shoe. An ugly metal filing cabinet to one side. Chairs like the ones Ricky Chan likes to throw around the ward. Only the Persian has survived. Doctor Petrakis has moved up the food chain since then.

I was different too. I answered Doctor Petrakis when she

asked me things. Sometimes she didn't even have to ask. I just told her. I chatted to the nurses. I didn't stab anyone in the face with a bishop from the chess set. They tailed off my meds. After four weeks, Doctor Petrakis and her colleagues decided I was good to go. They'd keep me one more week for observation, and that would be that. Just to make sure their decision was the correct one. I managed to keep all my faces handy back then. It kept them happy. Halfway through our last session, Doctor Petrakis called someone into the room. The someone was a young woman with wild blonde hair and little blue eyes. She sat in the chair furthest from me. As though I'd bite her or something.

"This is Sonia McFarlane," Doctor Petrakis said. "She's a friend of mine." Doctor Petrakis raised her eyebrows at me. As if to say, *What do you think?* As if this made the reason for the girl's presence clear. It didn't. Sonia McFarlane in a corner of the grey linoleum room. She fidgeted with her fingers. She was a lot younger than Doctor Petrakis. I wondered if she'd been a patient at some point.

"Hi, Sonia," I said.

She mumbled something and tried to smile.

"Sonia has agreed to do me a favour," Doctor Petrakis said. "She has created a position for you at the newspaper where she works. If you take it, you'll be on probation for three months. Just like any other employee. If everything goes well, it could turn into a permanent post. You'll have routine.

Something to do. An income. Independence. You could even finish your architectural studies by correspondence. What do you think?"

Sonia looked up at me and tried to smile again. She was a little more successful than before.

"I don't know what to say," I said to Doctor Petrakis.

"Though it's not my place to put words into your mouth," Doctor Petrakis said, "my suggestion would be that you say 'yes.'"

Doctor Petrakis stops staring at the chart. She flips Madge and Sonia away. "We'll come back to those," she says. "Now, what can you tell me about these?"

This page also has two pictures stuck to it. They aren't the originals. They're bigger. The one on the left is an Edwardian woman in profile. She has the jaw of a boxer. She's smiling. Laughing, even. Candidly. You didn't do that in the early 1900s. You scowled. Or at least tried to put your nothing face on as you sat rigid for the camera and waited long minutes for your face to stick to the film. To her right is a young woman in a red dress. There's the ghost of a plane behind her.

The copies aren't very good. They're pretty poor, actually. They look as if they've been lying under a hedge for a month. The Edwardian woman has a black eye. Fungus or mildew or something. There are brown and green stains. It's not a colour photograph.

The woman in red has suffered her own tribulations. Some of the pigment has been washed off. Seeing my photographs like that makes me want to throttle Doctor Petrakis. *My* photographs. Mine. Copied by a retard who managed to get his lunch all over Jaw Woman. His tea all over Woman in Red. All he has managed to do properly is increase their size. I can feel myself rising out of the chair. Doctor Petrakis has her back to me. She's holding a marker. Probably deciding which of the pictures to circle. I can be on her before she knows what's happened. Drive that marker through her neck. At the soft bit behind the jawbone and below the ear. I wonder if her husband would appreciate the enhancement.

I'm almost out of the chair when Mr. Naicker's judo sermon comes back to me. This must be what he was talking about. When they attack you. When you need to use their momentum against them. When you step aside and trip up the assailant. When you flash the cape at the bull. Doctor Petrakis circles Jaw Woman once. She hears the leather creak as I sit down again. She whips around.

"Are you all right, Nathan?" she asks. A frown flickers. I'm not sure which face I have on. She is about to sneeze. She suppresses it. She squeaks with the effort. "Excuse me," she says. Goes to her desk and takes a wad of tissues from her handbag. Peels off two. Blows. Balls them up. Wipes the end of her nose. Sniffs. It's not only revolting.

It's boring. She leans against the desk and crosses her ankles. "Who is the woman in the black-and-white photograph?" she asks.

I shrug. Nobody. Somebody. I don't know. It doesn't matter.

"Come, Nathan," she says. Sniffs. "We were doing so well."

I breathe in deeply, breathe out again. Unless I talk, I'll just sit here for the next half an hour. Then Johnson or September will be summoned to fetch me. Doctor Petrakis will make more tea and see her next patient. Or she'll go home to discuss the weather with her husband. And next time we'll be in the same place again.

"My great-great aunt," I say. "I didn't like her very much."

Doctor Petrakis frowns. The inside bits of her nostrils are wet. "This photograph must be a hundred years old," she says. What she's really saying is that I couldn't possibly have known the woman in the picture.

"I never liked her jaw. A jaw like that is ugly on a woman."

"I see," Doctor Petrakis says. I don't know what she sees.

"And she's laughing. It's not appropriate to the period. Photography wasn't snappy Instagram stuff back then. It was an occasion. You posed. You had to pose for, like, minutes at a time without moving. That's how film worked in those days. She would have had to hold that grin for a long time. It creeps me out."

"Why is that?" Doctor Petrakis asks. She dabs at her nostrils with a ball of tissues. The tissues are pink. I wonder if her house is all terracotta like the walls of her office. Or if it's all pink like her tissues.

"Because." I don't have the energy to explain. I take a deep breath. I throw her a reason. "Because she is going to so much effort to tell the world that she's a happy smiley person," I say.

"And you don't like that?"

"No. It makes me not believe her."

Doctor Petrakis sips at her tea. It's no longer steaming. It has no milk in it. It must still be warm. She draws a circle around Woman in Red. The circle overlaps the one around Jaw Woman. Like a Venn diagram that shows they share something.

"And who is this?"

I can't believe I've walked into this. She obviously knows who my mother is. My mother is an ageing nymphomaniac with her hair dyed the colour of honey. With her thinning lips painted a harlot's red. My mother is a liar and a thief. She lied to me. For me. About me. And stole just as much from me as Aunty Mike did. More, actually. I can't tell Doctor Petrakis that Woman in Red is my mother.

"I don't know," I say. I don't shrug. It's true. I don't know who she is. The truth can be a greased pig when you want it to be.

"So you have a photo of someone, and you don't know who it is," Doctor Petrakis says with a sniff. The sniffing is driving me nuts. I wish she'd stop. She's having one of her telepathic moments and blows her nose. Wipes it with the ball of tissues in her hand.

"I bought an old photo album from Madge, and that picture was in it. Loose between the pages. I liked it. I have no idea who she is."

She scribbles a few notes. I look at the image. Looking at it blown up like that is weird. The woman is more Rubenesque than I'd thought. Curvy. If her dress was yellow, she'd have looked like Mrs. du Toit that day I had a flat white with her. Seems the cretin who enlarged the picture got his ratios all wrong. Stretched her sideways. Broadened her shoulders. Widened her hips.

Doctor Petrakis steeples her hands and looks up at me. "Do you want to tell me about the pictures up on your wall?" she asks.

"Not really," I tell her.

MY NEXT SESSION is cancelled. Doctor Petrakis is ill. Actually, the whole ward is sniffing and sneezing and carrying on. Suddenly blowing your nose in a public place doesn't seem like such a bad idea.

"H1N1," Mr. Naicker says. "All it took was some Oriental fellow to sneeze on a plane and the whole world was in a panic. Did you know that the influenza pandemic of the twenties killed more people than the Great War?"

I did. I let him tell me anyway. He does, giving me the usual statistics. We're playing chess. It's taken us twenty minutes to advance a pawn each.

"And here we are," Mr. Naicker says by way of wrapping up his influenza lecture. "Locked up like battery chickens, each one making the other sick. How demeaning it would be to die of something as pedestrian as the flu."

As opposed to having your throat slit. Or being stabbed to death. Or being found dead behind your counter. Your tongue a thick white sausage between your lips. Contusions at your neck. Strands of pink silk clinging to it. Could Madge have survived the cancer? The question worries me, mostly at night when the rain blurs the moon at my window. I tell myself that she had no chance. She probably would have died by now anyway. Painfully. The cancer had infiltrated every organ of her body, she'd told me. After a while I believe myself. Then I can fall asleep.

Mr. Naicker has moved another pawn. He yawns. I can see his heart isn't in the game. He stops talking. I consider the board. I'd imagine a chessboard looks different each time to those who know what they're doing. It always looks the same to me. Eight by eight. My pieces about to march off down their well-trodden routes. I move a pawn. I look at Mr. Naicker. He has fallen asleep. His chin is on his chest and his saggy eyelids have closed. I put away the pieces. The empty board reminds me of the Chinese rice story. Where the emperor offers a man any reward of his choosing. The man asks for nothing more than a grain of rice on the first square of the chessboard. Two on the second. Four on the third. And so on, doubling the grains with each square. I've never tried the calculation. I try it now. I'm not even half-way when I stumble at ten billion-and-something grains of rice. The numbers are too big for me to keep in my brain. I stop. Exponential growth. I think that's what it's called. Maths never was a strong point. Perhaps that's why I don't get Ricky's sums. Seven and two and a half. Why he gets so excited about those figures. Maybe I should just ask. Now that I'm talking and all. I look around for him. He's slumped in a chair, staring at the television. His eyes blank. It's the wrong time to approach Ricky. I'm bored. I wonder if they've reduced my meds. I don't get bored when I'm stoned on their pills. Time doesn't matter then. I'd like to go for a run. And I'd kill for a beer.

I FIGHT WITH the breakfast porridge. It has the con-sistency of phlegm. Usually I shovel it down to make it go away. I'm scheduled to see Doctor Petrakis at ten. I treat each sticky spoonful as a measure of time. When the bowl is empty I still have an hour of waiting. I kill it by watching *The Simpsons* with Socks. He laughs at all the wrong moments, as usual. Doctor Petrakis looks pale. Her nose is covered with base. It's probably bright red underneath. The base looks almost like fur. She doesn't take off her scarf. She goes to the flipchart. Finds my pictures. Looks at Jaw Woman and Woman in Red for a while. Flips a sheet. Back to the page with Madge and Sonia. She takes the marker and draws a blue circle around Sonia.

"What was it like to work with Sonia?" she asks.

I shrug. This time it means I'm thinking. "Fine," I say. I sound like a teenager so I say some more. "Generally good. I think we were friends. Mostly."

Doctor Petrakis writes the word under Sonia's picture. Friends. Then she looks at me over her glasses.

"Until the end, I suppose," I add.

"Why 'until the end'?" she asks.

I shrug again. "Because she basically fired me, I suppose."

"So, before that you were friends?"

I stare at the carpet for a while. I scratch my face. It goes scritch scritch because I haven't been shaved for a day or two. "We'd get together after work at Eric's. Chat. We'd have a few beers. Sometimes lots."

Doctor Petrakis frowns. Smiles a tight little smile.

"Her boyfriend is an arsehole" I say. "He didn't like Eric's very much. He didn't like me very much either. In fact he liked me so little that I don't think he ever considered me a person. Let alone competition. I suppose that's why he tolerated Sonia and me going to Eric's together. Like a guy would tolerate his girlfriend socialising with a gay guy. We'd talk about work. About the people there. Have a laugh. Get really pissed sometimes too."

"Eric's?"

"A bar near the paper. Our local."

"And Sonia would also drink?"

"Usually. Mostly, I suppose. I don't know. I only saw her drink when I was there. So I don't know if she sat there drinking alone or with other people when I wasn't there."

Doctor Petrakis goes to her desk and scribbles a note on her pad.

"Did you have any other friends?"

"There was Madge. And Mrs. du Toit."

"Yes, there was. Were. We'll talk about them another time, shall we?"

"There was Eric. He was sort of a friend."

Doctor Petrakis sits down at her desk and looks at me.

"What do you remember about the day you were—about your last day at the paper?"

"Not much. I left."

"Did Sonia invite you to Eric's for a drink after work?"

I shrug. I shake my head. Together they mean I don't know.

"Did you go to Eric's for a drink?"

Shrug. Shake my head.

"Nathan, I really need you to tell me what you remember. About the evening after your last day at work."

I breathe in, breathe out. "I left the office. I didn't have a box of stuff like people in the movies who get fired. I had nothing at the office that was mine. I left. That's all I remember."

"So your last memory was leaving the office?"

"Yes."

"And what do you remember next?"

"Being here. Here in your office. You talking and me not."

This time Doctor Petrakis is the one to take a deep breath. She makes a duck face and sighs. I think she's going to call the end of the session. She doesn't. She speaks slowly. "How much time was there, do you think, between your last day at work and your coming here?"

I shrug. "A night," I say.

She writes long enough to write, "a night." Her eyebrows are up. "How did you get here?" she asks.

I'd never thought about that. I was there. Then I was here. How the fuck did I know how I got here? I forget things. I like to forget things. I stare at the carpet. It's looking a little like a jungle again. Doctor Petrakis picks up the phone, dials. "I need another half-hour," I hear her say. She puts down the phone. "Nathan, please try to think about the time between your last evening at the paper and the time you arrived here." She takes her glasses off and puts them on her desk. Sits back. Watches me.

I walked home. Up the hill. Past the laundry. Past Salie's café. Past the invisible buildings and cars and people on the way. Took the lift. Mrs. du Toit had gone away. No chance of meeting her on the way up. I looked for some of her wine in my flat. I knew there wouldn't be any. I sat on the couch. Sonia had gone away. Or maybe she hadn't. She'd invited me to Eric's. No hard feelings. A last friendly drink. After this she would go away. Definitely. I turned on the TV. I was hoping for rubbish alien documentaries. I watched some stuff about people buying other people's junk. And then I watched another programme about people trying to sell other people's junk. Someone paid a lot of money for a signed picture of Fatty Arbuckle. The old movie star was smiling. It must have been taken before his trouble with the dead actress. I could stick it on my wall and make Fatty Arbuckle my great-grandfather. I couldn't believe the next programme. It was about a whole different bunch of people buying junk from a completely different bunch. This time they rooted around in old sheds and trash. Like bergies on garbage day. Then they sold it to people who tried to sell it to other people. There was something strangely apocalyptic about it all.

It was dark out. The glow from the streetlights rose up to light my ceiling. The next programme was about people trying to replicate antique guns by using modern materials. No aliens. It was boring. I left the flat and walked down the hill to Eric's. I stopped at the window. Saw that there were only about four people inside. Eric was polishing glasses. Every now and then he yawned. If you knew Eric like I know Eric you'd know it was time to leave. He was big enough to swallow you whole. Probably would, just so he could close up. Two journos sat at the counter. Not Dino. And there sat Sarel and Sonia. The journos were a guy and a girl. The guy had his arm around the girl. Sarel had his wallet and keys in his hand. They were taking Eric's hint. They were about to leave. Then I saw Sarel say something. Sonia threw back her wild hair and laughed. I could hear her laugh through the glass. Sarel waved at Eric. He shambled over. He didn't look too happy. He shambled away again. The girl journo put her bag back on the counter. She scampered off. To the loo, I supposed. The boy journo followed her. Sarel watched them go. I could see him looking over Sonia's shoulder. He leant forward and whispered something. She whipped her head around to look where the journos had gone. Then she laughed again. Sarel was still in her face. She took his ears in her hands. She pulled him close. Kissed him. Backed off and shook her head. Sarel looked at her and took her face in his hands and kissed her. There was no more tossing. They kissed and kissed. For a second I felt for Dino. The second passed. Eric put two shooters on the counter. I wondered if he ever thought about me. Sonia and Sarel looked at Eric. Put their fingers to their lips. As if they were in a pantomime and Eric was the audience. Eric poked a fat finger at the bill on the table. Sarel paid. Said something to Sonia. They both looked towards the loos and laughed. Sonia shook her head. Then they downed their shooters and stood up. Sonia didn't look too sober. I needed to pee. I should have peed against a plane tree fifteen minutes earlier. Now it was too late. Sonia and Sarel were coming out. I stepped back, hid behind a skinny tree trunk. It was a ridiculous hiding place. They stopped and kissed again.

"Dino's going to kill you," Sonia said.

"Only if you let him."

"Your place, then?"

"Absolutely," said Sarel. "See you there."

They kissed again. I could hear the sucking of it from where I stood. Sarel put his hand on Sonia's crotch and squeezed. She moaned and almost doubled over and pushed him away. Then she laughed and said, "Wait!" and kissed him on the cheek and went left up St. George's Mall. Sarel went off to the right. I went after Sonia. She wasn't walking that straight.

I came up behind her. "Psst!" I hissed.

She squealed and jumped. For a moment I could see the whites of her eyes as well as the blue. "Jesus wept, Nathan," she said. "Fuck me if I didn't almost piss myself."

"Thought I'd walk you to your car," I said. "It's not that safe out here."

"Where the hell have you been, anyway?" she said as we walked.

"Here and there," I said. "I got to Eric's too late to join you. Sorry."

"No problem. Are you okay, Nate? After today and all, I mean?"

"I'm perfectly fine. I'm not so sure about you, though. Were you planning to drive?"

We're walking up Keerom Street. It's darker there. Deserted. Especially on a week day. I could feel Madge's scarf in my pocket. The silkiness turned greasy with all my fiddling. Sonia's arm was hooked into mine. She might have fallen over otherwise. She squinted up at me. She always squinted. She laughed.

"Of course I'm going to drive," she said.

"No you're not," I said.

Doctor Petrakis is still waiting. I don't think she's moved. Her glasses are still on the desk. Maybe she's scared of breaking my train of thought. Derailing the story. Shutting me up again. Negating the extra half-hour she's requested. She sees me looking at her. The eyebrows go up. "And?" she says.

I'm not going to answer. I don't care how I got here. Or how long it took. It's not important.

"I might have killed Sonia," I say.

THE BASIC DISTINCTION

"The basic distinction between sanity and insanity," Doctor Petrakis says, "is whether the accused knows right from wrong."

It's our last session before my trial. It's going to be a biggie, Ricky kept saying. Until his comes up of course. His will be much bigger. Of course. Bigger headlines too, he said. Flaying open the underbelly of violence that forms the pillars of South African society. And Mr. Naicker was worried about mixing metaphors. "We all want to kill every each one of us." That's a quote. From Ricky. I didn't know what he meant at the time. It was barely grammatical, even. So I leant over the entropy of the chess table and said, very quietly, "Why don't you shut the fuck up before I strangle you." Ricky looked like he'd seen a ghost. He pushed his chair back. It stuck on the linoleum again. He went over backwards. Again. The screaming and the nurses. They expected blood. There wasn't any.

They take me to court in an ambulance. I'm in a wheel-chair. Probably so that I can't run away. I have cuffs on my wrists. The cuffs are chained to the wheelchair. The wheelchair is chained to the floor of the ambulance.

It reminds me of a Negro spiritual. I'm not sure if you can still say "Negro." I can't remember all the words. Something about head-bones connecting to neck-bones. I remember the tune. It's not a tune that's easy to forget. Even for me. It sticks in my head the whole way. The neck-bone's connected to the—head-bone. Over and over. I try to forget it. I can't. There are people outside the court. They're shouting and waving placards. The placards say things about the death penalty. About bringing it back. There must be another big trial on today.

"Don't stress, my guy," Johnson says. I'm not, though. Even if this might be my first day on the journey to prison. I don't know why I'm not stressing.

He wheels me down the corridors. The paint is peeling. There are potholes in the linoleum. There's a smell of feet and stale cigarette smoke. There are no-smoking signs everywhere. I'm being looked at. Stared at. Whispered about behind cupped hands. I put on my retard face to give them more to talk about. My jaw hangs open and my head tilts to one side and my eyes go all squiffy.

Doctor Petrakis is standing outside Court Six. When she sees me her eyebrows fly up and her eyes widen. "Nathan!" she hisses. I feel as if I'm one of her children. There are two men with her. The younger one has a long thin face. An undershot jaw. A cape over his shoulders that reaches almost to the floor. The older man also wears a cape. He leans on a stick. His back is bowed. He has an amazing amount of hair in his ears. They are big and meaty and lie flat against his head. His eyebrows haven't been trimmed since about 1979. Doctor Petrakis continues to scowl at my retard face.

"Enough of that, Nathan," she says. "This is Advocate McEwan and counsel Mr. Carver." Both men nod. I don't know which is which. The old man puts out a hand. Withdraws it when he sees my cuffs. And my face, too, probably.

"Nathan," he says. He grunts as if he's tired, or sore somewhere. "Here we are, son."

I don't know what he wants with me. I put on my nothing face. I look at Doctor Petrakis. "Are you my friend, Aphrodite?" I ask. I've never called her Aphrodite before. I'm sure she asked me to call her that a long time ago.

"What do you think?" she says. Therapists. They can never answer a question without turning it back on you. Always penetrating your most private bits. *The rapists.* I pity her husband. What would you like to do this weekend, Aphrodite dear? What would *you* like to do, darling husband? Just imagine.

"Do you really want to know what I think?" I say to Doctor Petrakis.

"Nathan, I've been trying for months to know what you think." She puts a hand on my shoulder. Smiles. I could eat that smile. Chew those lips off her. I am handcuffed to the chair. I wonder if she's even close to knowing what I think. Such a closed and secret place, the brain. Impenetrable. Even for a dedicated rapist.

"What I think is that we're all insane," I say. Her eyebrows go up. The men in their Batman capes look at each other. I carry on before she can ask why I think that. "In varying degrees. We're all a little madder than the one sitting next to us. All of us somewhere on the spectrum of bonkers." Birds on a wire, sitting wing to wing. The increments of madness so small, from one to the other.

I AM ACCUSED

I am accused of the attempted murder of Sonia McFarlane. Who, the prosecutor points out, was saved by the timely arrival of one Sarel Theron. Who had placed his car keys in the victim's handbag for safekeeping, and had forgotten to retrieve them on leaving the bar. Ms McFarlane, the prosecution would show, was in the process of being strangulated with the aid of a scarf, pink or thereabouts in colour, by the accused. Had Mr. Theron not arrived, Ms McFarlane would not have survived.

I wonder whether "strangulated" is a real word. And whether the correct "process" was being followed by the accused at the time.

I am accused of the murder of Madge Cartwright. The cause of death strangulation, the instrument a silk garment or piece of fabric, pink or thereabouts in colour.

I am accused of the murder of one Constable Annette de Villiers, whose body was found in the Company's Gardens, her biker boots protruding from a bush. On her person was found a black-and-white Edwardian-era photograph of a woman with features not unlike her own. The postmortem revealed that Constable de Villiers had also been strangulated. Though more effectively, it was clear, than Ms McFarlane.

I am accused of the murder of one Adele du Toit, whose car was discovered in Woodstock, and whose body was found in a ravine off Tafelberg Road.

Beneath Mrs. du Toit's body was found a photograph, dating to the early 1970s, of a woman wearing a red dress, standing at what appeared to be an airfield, who bore a notable resemblance to the deceased. The post mortem found that Mrs. du Toit had also been strangulated. My fingerprints were all over the car, inside and out.

My place is supposed to be in the dock. I don't know if it's called a dock here. I'm going by Hollywood. The dock is raised. It's narrow. Along the side facing the judge there are microphones. I'm not in the dock because my wheelchair won't fit. Johnson has wheeled me up next to it. I'm blocking the little flappy door that leads to the pit where the lawyers and officials sit. From where I am, I look over a sunken area full of people. I show a man in police uniform my retard face. He looks away. On the other side is the judge. Old Mr. Carver sits with his back to me. The younger man is standing at a microphone. His hair has begun to thin at his crown. I wonder if he's noticed this. Whether anyone has pointed it out to him. He is listening to a woman who stands to the left of the judge. The woman is making the accusations. She also has a microphone. It

MY NAME IS NATHAN LUCIUS

isn't working. She looks about twelve. She is Indian. She has a dot on her forehead between her eyes. There's a mystique in it that makes her more beautiful. She's been talking all the while. I struggle to make out what she's saying.

All the women, the Indian woman at the microphone says—Madge Cartwright, Annette de Villiers and Adele du Toit—had been strangulated with the same pink (or cerise or crimson or rose, depending upon interpretation) silk scarf. She produces a plastic bag stuffed with Madge's scarf. She calls it Exhibit One. Said scarf, the state would show, was found on my person after the McFarlane incident. Even from here I can see how filthy Exhibit One is. Madge would be horrified.

The Indian woman sits down. She flicks a look at me. I can see she doesn't like me very much. I suppose I can understand why. I don't care. The judge writes something down and turns a page. Then she says something to Mr. McEwan. The judge is so far away that I can't hear her. Her microphone isn't working either. Mr. McEwan replies. He has his back to me. I can't hear him. Mumble mumble mumble, he goes. He leans into a microphone. It seems his is also out of order. I'm not expected to say anything. Just to sit there. An exhibit. Evidence that I exist. Everyone stands when the judge stands. I can't stand, of course. I'm chained to the wheelchair. The judge leaves the courtroom. Some people sit down again. Others turn to look at me. Some begin talking to each other. Everyone begins to file out slowly. The room smells of dust and armpit and faraway cigarettes.

"DID I REALLY kill those women?" I ask Doctor Petrakis. The sky is a thick dark blue. It presses on her window. I wonder if the glass will withstand the pressure of all that blueness. If not the window will burst inwards. We'll both be drowned by sky if it does.

"You tell me, Nathan," she says. Her cold has gone. There's coffee in her mug. Not some or other citrus tea. I wonder if she'll ever call me Nate. Like Madge used to. And Sonia.

"I'm not talking about Madge," I say. She knows I killed Madge. She knows why I did it. I know she knows. I told her.

"Nor am I," Doctor Petrakis says. You see now, I want to say to her. You weren't talking at all. Not about anyone. You've done that thing again.

"I feel like K.," I say.

"Who?"

"K."

Perhaps she isn't very well read. Or else she's just doing the shrink thing.

"K. who is arrested and put on trial. And never knows what he's accused of."

She screws her eyes up and tilts her head to one side. Huh? her face says.

"Come on, Aphrodite," I say. It's nice to tell *her* to come on for a change. It's nice to use her first name. "Kafka. The ultimate paranoiac. I hope you've read him."

"'Paranoiac' isn't a term we use any more," she says. I'm not concerned about scientific or political correctness right now. It's a label. A simple descriptor. Like the "tall" woman or the "fat" man. Everyone knows they would have other attributes too. You can't go through life simply being tall or fat. You need other things to get by. Describing them like that is just shorthand. Otherwise we would spend our lives describing people who aren't really worth it. Kafka was paranoiac. Paranoid. Or just plain scared. Or not, and just made up everything he wrote. What do I know? I'm not a shrink. Whatever Kafka was, he wrote K.'s story of the trial. I don't say anything. Doctor Petrakis is also silent for a while. Sips her coffee. Pokes at her pad. Sometimes her coyness irritates. I know her well enough by now. She's not writing anything. Just poking. Dabbing ink on the page. Making space to think.

"There's a difference, Nathan," she says. Finally. "K. didn't know what he was on trial for. You do."

"Does it count if I don't remember anything?"

"Your photographs were on the scene. One with each woman."

"You can't know right from wrong if you don't remember anything."

I'M WHEELED INTO the courtroom for further sessions. Each one takes up an entire day. Sometimes we just wait around and nothing happens. We go back. Home, I almost said. Court is supposed to start at 9 am. Sometimes it only starts at 10. If at all. Then it goes on for an hour or so. Then there's recess. Sometimes recess runs into the lunch hour. When it does, court resumes at 2 pm. Sometimes 2:30 pm. At 3 pm the judge grants an adjournment.

We're all outside the courtroom one day. The old man is sitting on a wooden bench. His hands are folded around the crook of his walking stick. Doctor Petrakis—Aphrodite to her friends—is next to him. Johnson is leaning against a wall. I'm in the wheelchair.

"Mr. McEwan," I say to the younger man in the cape. He takes a step back. Almost jumps. "Why all the late starts and recesses?" I ask him anyway. Mr. McEwan says nothing.

The old guy laughs. He looks at me. If you took away the folds of skin that pressed on his eyelids he would look like a mischievous schoolboy. His eyes shine through shaggy brows. Through his spectacles. The skin around them makes them smaller than Sonia's. Still, I can see that they're blue. Or grey. Or green. Or a bit of all of that.

It's the first time I've looked into them. They're clean and clear. They hide nothing. There's no guile in them. No oblique strategies. No bullshit. They laugh easily. I like Mr. Carver. He puts his elbows on his knees and leans closer. "Because that is the judicial process these days." He sighs. Grunts. Shakes his head. "The judicial process these days," he says again.

SO

"So," Mr. Naicker says. My trial has been going on for ever. Sometimes it goes on without me. Spring flowers have erupted on verges. Trees have begun to bud. Mr. Carver tells me that yet another prosecutor has been appointed. It's the third. The woman prosecutor got pregnant. There was morning sickness. I wonder if her baby will be born with a dot on its forehead. Her replacement was a man who came to court drunk. Mr. Carver says the drunk man told the judge to go and fuck her hand. After he was arrested they found six empty beer cans and a half-jack of vodka in his car. Mr. Carver laughs. The new prosecutor needs time to go through the material. He is clearly a slow reader. Mr. Carver says he's had fifty-five years of this kind of thing. He says it's nothing short of a miracle that he doesn't have a bed next to mine and his own daily meds to swallow.

"I know what you're going through," Mr. Naicker continues. "I personally thought I might die before I saw some kind of resolution. It's variable, you know." He moves his knight. His finger is still on it. That lets me know he's still contemplating the move. It allows him to move it back to where it was. And then to consider another move. That's precisely what he does. I'm waiting to hear what exactly it is that is "variable." Mr. Naicker is thinking about his move. I'm thinking about kicking him on the shin. Kicking those wormy veins to get him going. At last he leaves his knight alone. I contemplate a pawn.

"Take Ricky, for instance," Mr. Naicker says. "When did you last see Ricky?"

I think about this. I don't know. It seems like a long time ago. I shrug.

"Well, our friend Ricky got the judicial fast-track. They considered him completely compos mentis. Perfectly capable of standing trial. Perfectly capable of suffering the punishment. So." He moves his bishop. Keeps his finger on the mitre. Looks at the piece from one angle. Then another. "So," he says, "Ricky got seven life terms. Consecutive. One for each of his victims. To be served at a regular correctional institution. Which means getting regularly buggered, regularly beaten up and regularly stabbed. For the rest of his natural life." Mr. Naicker takes his finger off his bishop. Sits back.

Now Ricky's maths makes sense. Seven for him. Mrs. du Toit, the constable and Sonia make it two and a half for me. If he'd known about Madge, he'd have been a lot more impressed.

"It will be a miracle if Ricky survives even one of his life sentences. We are the lucky ones, Nathan," he says. "We crazies get to play chess and drink coffee out of paper cups. We are warm and dry and we are fed and watered. Drugged when the authorities believe we need to be. We don't have to concern ourselves with businesses or careers. They trim our beards and clip our toenails and make sure we see the dentist. We have no responsibilities or obligations. On the contrary, we get to compile our mental troubles as one might compose an email. We hit 'send' and they land in the inboxes of Doctors Humboldt, Petrakis et al." He watches as I consider the release of my queen. "We have the channels of catharsis at our disposal. We can simply take the worst of ourselves and hand it over politely to willing recipients who have strings of clever letters behind their names. Then we sleep soundly while the good doctors dream our nightmares for us. And the next morning we get to do it all over again."

I move my queen to threaten attack Mr. Naicker's bishop. He nudges it out of danger. "Perhaps we're not the crazy ones after all," he says.

THE SHUFFLING OF PAPER

The shuffling of paper is never-ending. Doctor Petrakis will testify that I am not fit for prison. Those are her words. What they mean is she'll testify that I am crazy. That I should be held at a psychiatric facility for the foreseeable future. The phrase implies that somebody, somewhere, has the ability to foresee the future. I don't press the point.

Before she gets her chance I have to listen to a string of other witnesses. It goes on for weeks. I'm fine with that. I'm not in a hurry. There are only two possible outcomes. It's like playing chess with Mr. Naicker. I'll either win or lose.

Inspector Morris is the first to make a move. He describes finding Madge and the other women. He does this in great detail. He is surprisingly detached. I try to put images to his words. Sounds, smells. Weather. Ambient temperatures. I can't. It's like listening to someone telling you about a movie you haven't watched. The pictures you conjure up are nothing like what they've seen. I do remember one thing, though. I remember the days after Aunty Mike and the woodshed. When Mom answered the phone. When she told her friends that the week on the lake had been idyllic. When she gushed about a holiday that was nothing like she said it was. All sunshine and family fun. Inspector Morris was doing exactly that. Telling a story in which I didn't appear. Where my truth had no place. A tight and considered lie. Like Mom's.

I'd been right about Morris. He wasn't stupid. Not that you had to be a genius to see the insanity defence coming. Or clairvoyant. Morris didn't need to see my counsel's files to know what they'd planned. So he didn't dwell on Constable de Villiers or Mrs. du Toit or Sonia. He homed right in on Madge. Only a sane person, he said, and a very cunning one at that, would have the capacity to create an alibi out of an innocent customer, a young computer programmer whose girlfriend loved tortoises. Only a very cunning and totally sane person would be able to hoodwink an experienced investigative team for so long. That was not the mark of a deranged person. Inspector Morris went red when he told the next part of his story. How I'd appeared on the security cameras as I left the shop. How I'd gone around the back. How I'd waited for the customer to leave before throttling Madge. He went a deeper red when Mr. McEwan got him to admit that this was all pure speculation. That I'd appeared at the police station of my own accord. That I had offered to give them my fingerprints. That he had then let me go without pressing any charges.

"So am I insane or not?" I ask Mr. McEwan afterwards. I'm not comfortable with what Inspector Morris had to say. We're walking down the corridor. They're walking, at least. I'm being pushed in a wheelchair by Johnson. Every now and then we stop so that Mr. Carver can catch up.

"Don't you worry about a thing," Mr. McEwan says. He doesn't look at me. I look up at Doctor Petrakis. She's staring straight ahead. Down the corridor, past the wasted beings that populate the place. Bags of skin filled with bad decisions and uncertain futures.

THE NEXT TIME they call a few witnesses from the biker bar. Two customers and the barman appear. They each have a few minutes to point me out. To confirm that I had been drinking with Annette de Villiers. The barman contradicts the customers. He insists that I'd ordered only two beers, and that the first had hardly been touched when it spilled. He remembers that I barely touched the second one. That he was irritated by my drinking free tap-water all night. The prosecutor asks him why he should remember such an arbitrary thing. "In my line of work, it's pretty memorable when people don't drink the drinks they've bought," he says. The gallery titters.

The drunk guy with the fake German accent doesn't appear. I'm disappointed. I'd told Mr. Carver about him. I was looking forward to watching him being put in his place by Mr. McEwan.

THE DAY IT'S Sonia's turn she's full of tears. Her little eyes are swollen almost shut. She turns her face from me. She struggles to talk. Eventually the prosecution gets the story out of her. I'd walked with her for a bit, she says. I asked her if she was intending to drive. She'd said yes. Then I told her she wasn't. She thought I was going to offer to drive her home. Then I jumped her. Wound the scarf around her neck. Just before she passed out she realised what I'd meant. When I told her she wasn't going to drive. No, she had no idea why I'd tried to kill her. Other than having just fired me, which she'd done in the nicest possible way.

She is asked some more questions, mostly about work. I stop listening. I know all that. It's boring. I try to scratch my nose with my shoulder. It's itchy at the tip and driving me crazy.

When they call pathologists and other specialists, I stop listening. It's the movie thing again. A story told by other people, with someone else in the starring role. I don't remember killing Mrs. du Toit. Can't remember getting her to her car. Or dumping her in a ravine on Table Mountain. Driving her car to Woodstock. Cleaning her flat so thoroughly that you could eat off the floor. The state doesn't know how I got home after dumping the car. They're still trying to track down taxis who might have given me a lift. The prosecutor points out that I could simply have walked. The damp running clothes that I didn't understand now make sense. I didn't walk. I ran. I could tell them. Tell them that I ran all the way to town and up the hill to Tamboerskloof that night. Tell them that I washed my kit in Mrs. du Toit's washing machine.

The trouble is that nobody asks me.

THE WORST

The worst is when Doctor Petrakis takes the stand. She puts on a face I've never seen before. When she looks at me she may as well be looking at a street pole or a hubcap. Her consonants click and hiss like precision-engineered metal. She uses medical phrases. I only know some of them. I stop listening once I lose track. She's talking about parts of me I don't understand. It's like a physician going on about your patella or your epiglottis. When all you want to know is how your kneecap or your throat is doing.

Then she begins about the lake house. I can't stop listening any longer. I'm hearing. I don't want to. I want to cover my ears with my hands. My wrists are in cuffs. The cuffs are cuffed to the arms of the wheelchair. The arms are bolted to the wheelchair. The wheelchair is stuck to the earth by gravity. The earth spins in space. It flies around the sun. It's too big for me to stop. Someone begins moaning. It's not so much a moaning as a high flat keening. It sounds like a counter-tenor who has had a stroke and woken up tone-deaf. Doctor Petrakis stops talking. She looks down at her hands. The judge bangs her gavel. Words come out of her mouth. I can't hear them over the noise. She has her angry face on. I suppose her words are angry too. Johnson wheels me out. The shrieking person follows us into the corridor. Past people carrying signs about serial killers and death penalties. Into the ambulance. All the way home.

I DON'T FEEL like talking any more. I've talked and talked and look where that's got me. I should have just shut the fuck up in the first place. I consider telling this to Doctor Petrakis. That would be talking. I keep quiet. I'm sitting on the chair in her office. I'm sitting so still that there's not the slightest squeak. I don't need to look at the window to know that the southeaster is howling. The window rattles in its frame. Every so often a gust of wind is so strong I can feel the pressure change in my ears. I'm looking at the carpet. It whirls and curls and the red zings against the blue. Doctor Petrakis pulls a chair close to mine. She sits down.

"Nate," she says.

She just called me Nate. I wish I could find my smiling face. It's too much hard work to look for it.

"How are you handling the stress?" She waits for me to answer. I don't.

"We've had a chat to the judge," she says. "By 'we' I mean Mr. Carver and Mr. McEwan. They've got her to agree to exclude you from the rest of the proceedings. It's not as though you were going to take the stand anyway. They convinced her that having you there would disrupt the court too much. She didn't need much convincing after the last session. Are you okay with that?"

I shrug.

"I really need you to say yes or no. I can't have you excluded unless you allow it."

Twirls and swirls and furls.

"We have to call your mother as a witness. And possibly your sister too. Do you want to be there for that?"

Uncurl, untwirl, unfurl. Eventually I drag my eyes away. I shake my head. It loosens my tongue.

"No, I don't," I say.

BEFORE AND AFTER

IT'S ALL

It's all over.

Or perhaps it's just begun.

The court has decided that I am guilty. Guilty in that I did it. In that I murdered Madge, Mrs. Du Toit and Annette de Villiers. Not culpable, because I'm insane. So I'm not joining Ricky. I'm not being sent to a place where I'll be fucked up the bum again. I'm staying here. Probably for ever. Home. They'll be scared to let me out again. Look what happened the last time.

"Your move," I remind Mr. Naicker. He's used to me talking now. So are September and Johnson and all the rest. That first time I held my fists out and said, "You choose," Mr. Naicker almost jumped out of his chair.

"Oh my word, Nathan," he'd said. "You just scared the living bejesus out of me."

"Left or right?" I'd repeated.

Mr. Naicker got it. He got that he shouldn't make a big deal of it. He put a shaky hand on my left fist. He'd chosen white. Then he said, "It's a little blustery out. Still, maybe we can persuade Johnson to give us a whirl around the garden. What do you say?"

These days, it's much easier to find my smiling face.

WE SPOKE TO each other every day, Mr. Naicker and I. Until the day we ran out of things to say. The chess pieces stood idle between us. It was awkward. Things were probably easier when I wasn't speaking. When Mr. Naicker just babbled on and on. With neither of us under the pressure of holding an actual conversation.

So I asked him how he'd landed up here. Mr. Naicker went rigid. He stared at me. Stared and stared. I wished I'd kept my mouth shut.

Then he relaxed a little. "What have you heard?" he said.

I told him what Ricky Chin had said to me.

Mr. Naicker nodded as he listened. The nodding seemed to relax him. By the end of it he was more or less back to normal. He had one correction. His daughter hadn't been discussing her day at the consulting firm. She had been describing a Prada handbag in great and loving detail. To Mr. Naicker this seemed an important distinction. I wondered whether she'd still be alive if she'd chatted about work instead.

"And you, Nathan? What is your story?" Mr. Naicker said.

I'd opened the door, I realised. He already knew it all, or

pretty much, at least. There are no secrets in this place. I had no corrections for him. Their version seemed accurate enough. I have to go by what other people have to say on the matter. I don't have much to go on myself. Afterwards, Mr. Naicker and I agreed not to revisit our pasts. This means we can chat about anything. So our discussions frequently revolve around Ricky's talent for digging up information. We conclude our talks by inventing careers in which Ricky might have shone. Careers that don't involve seven gratuitous and wildly violent murders. A brilliant investigative journalist, perhaps. An archaeologist. A forensic auditor. A lawyer. A researcher of the obscure and arcane. A spy. Sometimes we share analyses about new inmates. It's not important if we're accurate or not. The stories we make up are entertaining enough. When we have nothing to talk about we simply shut up. That's fine as well.

MY DAYS ARE simple. I wake up. I get fed breakfast and my meds for the day. They've got the meds just right. I'm here and I'm not. I play chess with Mr. Naicker. I watch Socks Ferreira rock, or Old Man Jakes drool. There are no surprises, mostly. When there are, they usually take the form of a new arrival. There are two kinds of new arrival. Those who kick and scream. And those who don't. Both types make for good stories.

Other surprises occur on a more random basis. For

example, from time to time the orange-haired fellow goes ballistic and does a Ricky Chin. We all watch while Johnson and September wrestle him to the ground. Nobody has quite figured out what sets him off. That's what makes it surprising, I suppose.

I have lunch. I watch TV. I read books that Doctor Petrakis lends me.

"How did you feel after you finished *The Road*?" she says one day. I shrug. I'm talking again. A shrug's easier. I'm not trying to be difficult.

"I really don't know," I say. "Very similar to how anyone feels after they finish a book, I suppose. Sleepy, mostly."

"Weren't you moved by the lengths the father goes to in caring for his son?"

I shrug again. This time I don't say anything. I don't know much about protective fathers. Or mothers.

Sometimes I think of Madge. I try not to. It makes me sad. I miss her.

I think of Mrs. du Toit and the crazy things we got up to. It makes me horny. When my meds allow it. I try to feel sorry for what I did to her. I can't. She was leaving. Going away from me. Anyway, I wasn't there at the time I killed her. You'd remember something like that if you were there.

Sometimes I think of Sonia and Sarel and the rest trying to sell ad space to people who want it less and less. I bet they're still at it. I'm sure it's the same thing every day.

Sonia bitching at her troops. One thing, two things. So not very different to my days, actually. They're the hamsters on the wheel. Their job is to keep the wheel spinning. Here, the wheel runs without us. We don't have to do anything to make it turn. It's turned for us. I wonder if Sonia would like the drugs they give you in here. I hope she doesn't hate me too much.

I have supper. It's like the aeroplane food I had once. I swallow my pills without arguing. There are only a few these days. Not even a proper handful. I sleep. Sleeping is possibly the highlight of my day. I know that sounds sad. It's not. As long as there's no dark and no pine needles, each sleep is a triumph. I sleep like a drunkard. Even though the nights are now hot and humid. Even though mosquitoes find their way into my room. I still have the special concession of a private ward. I don't talk about it in case somebody notices. I am allowed to sleep with the light on. It's a bright white neon. I don't mind. I've never slept better.

I STILL SEE Doctor Petrakis. These days she sits on the chair next to me. Aphrodite is the goddess of love. Petrakis comes from petros, which is Greek for stone. When I point this out to her she puts her head to one side and smiles. It isn't a real smile. I don't suppose I'd just given her new information.

"What do you think that means, Nate?" she says.

"Not everything has to mean something," I say. "Sometimes things just are."

I DON'T SEE her as often as I used to. I think we're down to one session a week. I'm trying to persuade myself that she's not going away.

It's hard to understand weeks in here. One day is like the next or the one before. Most of us don't bother to think about time passing. There are a lot of things we don't need to think about here. And we don't really need weeks. Or weekends. A Sunday is as good as a Wednesday to a crazy person.

It's perfect.

Almost.

"Tell me more about the murders they say I committed," I say to Doctor Petrakis when we get together again.

"What do you want to know?" she asks. I'm fine with the answers coming back as questions now. I no longer want to chew my hand off in frustration. Or bite the inside of my cheeks until they bleed. She stands up and pulls a chair close to mine. She brings an aroma of jasmine and lemons with her. Summer means no more scarf. No whispering stockings. The pool at her Rondebosch house must be sparkling now. Clear and leaf-free. She crosses her sun-browned legs at the ankles. She balances her notepad on a knee.

"Is there any way at all that someone else might have committed those murders?"

She doesn't answer. She's probably thinking up another question.

"Apart from Madge's, of course," I say to give her time. "We both know I did Madge."

She frowns. Opens her mouth and closes it.

"Only because she asked me to," I remind her.

She opens her mouth again.

"Why do you ask, Nate?"

"Because I don't feel guilty about them. I don't feel bad. I don't feel anything. As far as I'm concerned I wasn't even there. I just want to know if it's irrefutable." *Refuted* doesn't mean counter-argued or disputed. Many people think it does. Especially journalists like Dino. Refuted means disproved, totally and utterly.

Doctor Petrakis gets it. "There will always be grey areas, Nate."

"Come on, Aphrodite. I'm not looking for appeasement here. I just want to know if there's a sliver of a chance that it wasn't me."

"Why?"

"Because if there is, it means the guy who really did it might still be out there."

Doctor Petrakis looks at me. She sighs.

"Nate, they found your DNA. Your fingerprints. You had

a proven connection with each of the women. Nobody on earth was connected to each of them the way you were. The way they were killed, which was exactly how you tried to kill Sonia, and how you had killed Madge. Fibres from Madge's scarf on their skin. The photographs you left with the bodies. Those very, very specific, unique photographs. There is just no way someone else could have done it."

She sounds like she's channelling the gentle Mr. Carver.

"Thank God for that," I say.

MY NAME IS NATHAN LUCIUS

My name is Nathan Lucius. I am thirty-two years old. I used to run. I don't know if I was running from something or towards it. Now I play chess. Every day I wake up into a world that is exactly the same as it was the day before. Whatever the season or the weather or the day of the week, every day is the same. I don't have to run to get there. Or away from it. I like it. It means I never have to remember anything. Or forget anything. Ever again.

"I wonder if there are holes in my brain," I say to Doctor Petrakis one day, mostly because I have nothing else to say. She's sitting close enough for me to see what she's writing. Her legs are even browner. *Holes in the brain?* she's written. She's underlined *Holes* twice. I know what she's going to say. She says it.

"What makes you say that, Nate?"

What makes me say that is, it's a whole new game to play with Doctor Petrakis.

"In each hole there's a tiny glass jar. In one, for instance, Mrs. du Toit is floating. In a red dress and red shoes. Not as a foetus, you understand. As Mrs. du Toit. There's no umbilical cord. Just Mrs. du Toit suspended in some fluid in a jar in a hole in my brain. Completely isolated from the rest of me. Insulated. Unconnected. Disconnected. And all the others, each in their separate jars floating in their own fluid. Each a separate jar in a separate hole in my brain. With no connection to one another."

Doctor Petrakis tilts the pad away from me. She's writing. I wonder if you can teach yourself to figure out what someone is writing by watching the other end of the pen. She's got it wrong again. She hasn't asked the question. The question is "Why?"

I answer it anyway. I put my sincere face on. "I need to resolve the not-remembering somehow," I say.

She looks up. There's a less than professional wetness in her eyes. The wrinkles at their corners have deepened. I suppose I've been more than a little trying. She lowers her pen. She is more beautiful than ever.

"Oh, Nate," she says. She reaches out and almost puts her hand on my knee. She retracts it and puts it to her chest, just below her throat.

Exactly where her scarf will be when winter comes around again.

ACKNOWLEDGMENTS

MY THANKS ARE due to Rachel McDermott and Dr. Kevin Stoloff for invaluable advice relating to mental health issues. All blunders in this regard are mine alone.

I am grateful to Julian Snitcher and Paul Warmeant, who offered encouragement when I needed it most.

Thanks are also due to my tenacious agent, James Woodhouse, and to my imperturbable editor, Lynda Gilfillan, for so calmly making molehills out of mountains.

As always, I am indebted to my wife, Michelle, and to our girls, for putting up with my own peculiar brand of madness that descends when I'm writing.